DISCARDED

GARRISON'S BOUNTY

Wes Garrison was but a name to Sheriff Ben Walls of Papago. But then a local cowman revealed the story of Indian Fort, its troubled history and Garrison's part in it. Driven by curiosity, Walls witnesses two killings and an unnatural death. Worse than that he comes within an ace of being killed himself. Only the tall midwife from Papago saves him. Despite all this he continues his investigation.

JOHN HUNT

GARRISON'S BOUNTY

Complete and Unabridged

LINFORD
Leicester

First published in Great Britain in 1997 by
Robert Hale Limited
London

First Linford Edition
published 1997
by arrangement with
Robert Hale Limited
London

British Library CIP Data

Hunt, John, *1916* –
    Garrison's bounty.—Large print ed.—
Linford western library
1. Western stories
2. Large type books
I. Title
813.5′4 [F]

ISBN 0–7089–5138–4

Published by
F. A. Thorpe (Publishing) Ltd.
Anstey, Leicestershire

Set by Words & Graphics Ltd.
Anstey, Leicestershire
Printed and bound in Great Britain by
T. J. International Ltd., Padstow, Cornwall

This book is printed on acid-free paper

1

A Sickening Sight

AFTER Sheriff Ben Walls returned, driving the liveryman's light spring wagon with the canvas-shrouded dead man in the back, several townsmen followed him to the livery-barn where a grim-faced liveryman removed the stud-necked mare from between the shafts and led her away, the questions began.

Initially no one had fully believed the itinerant horse trader who had come into town, put up his animals at the public corrals and after two jolts of Murphy's popskull had said, "I seen my share of dead ones but as Gawd's my witness I never seen anything like it up yonder. Whoever killed him didn't just shoot the feller, he went to work on him with rocks, wood clubs an' a knife."

The customers of Murphy's saloon were silent. The horse trader called for another whiskey which Murphy supplied, and, as the trader put a silver coin atop the bar, he blew out a ragged breath before continuing, "That poor feller warn't hardly recognizable as a human bein'. I seen what In'ians done but this was worse. One hell of a lot worse."

Someone asked if the trader found any papers on the dead man. He shook his head. "Didn't look for none. Didn't go no closer'n fifteen feet."

After the horse trader told the sheriff his story he got his trading stock on the road and left Papago without looking back. No one knew his name, no one had asked and it didn't matter.

By the time the sheriff returned with the spring wagon the story had spread throughout town. When a skinny tall man with a prominent Adam's apple asked Ben Walls at the livery-barn for details, Ben looked at the skinny tall man and shook his head.

He dragooned three townsmen to help him carry the weighty canvas shroud over behind the general store to the ice house. They left it there, the others dispersed and Sheriff Walls entered the emporium from the alley loading dock, hunted up the proprietor, Jared Whipple, and told him what he had done. Whipple, accustomed to having his ice house used for articles needing freezing, simply nodded his head and as the lawman left Whipple went to wait on a woman shopper.

Not until early evening, close to the time Whipple locked up for the night, did he know what Ben had put in his ice house. By that time every scrap of information that had surfaced after the horse trader had entered the saloon, had been passed by word of mouth throughout town. Jared Whipple stared at the tall, skinny man who told him, went around back to see for himself, even turned the shroud back a little. When he got home for supper he had no appetite.

The following morning Ben Walls visited the ice house. The corpse was as stiff as a ramrod. He hardened his resolve and proceeded to rummage through the corpse's pockets, a sickening business but it had to be done. He took what he had found inside the dead man's hat to the jailhouse to sift through his sticky findings which got steadily more sticky as the thaw set in.

The tall, skinny man who served Papago as local carpenter and handyman, Josh Whatly, came directly from the café to the jailhouse, Ben Walls's first visitor of the day. He considered the array of bloody articles on the sheriff's desk, turned and departed without a word.

Ben didn't blame him, some of the things from the dead man's pockets had thawing pieces of meat attached to them.

Jared Whipple crossed from his store shortly after the handyman had left, looked at the gory array on Ben's desk,

4

chose a chair across the room, sat down and said, "Ben, you can't keep him in there. Womenfolk come to buy ice."

The sheriff leaned back gazing at the storekeeper. "It's summer, Jared. Where else can I keep him?"

"Bury him," Whipple replied. "The sooner the better."

Ben nodded and the storekeeper arose, speaking as he went to the door. "Josh'll make the box, Murphy can send a pair of his steadies to dig the grave."

After Whipple's departure the sheriff returned to his unpleasant task of sifting through the articles on his desk. One thing bothered him, when he had examined what had been left of the dead man he had found no weapons and no horse. He assumed whoever had killed the stranger had appropriated these things. Two weeks later after the mangled carcass had been buried and local interest had turned to other things, a cowman named Ellis Snowden made the long ride from his ranch miles west of town leading a gaunt, rough looking bay horse. He put the animal in one of the public corrals, gave the liveryman two bits to grain and hay him, then went up to the sheriff's office.

When the greetings had been exchanged Ellis Snowden, an eminently practical individual who never rushed into anything, got comfortable on a bench and said, "One of my riders found a horse couple days back. Saddled and bridled but with both reins busted half way to the bit. We took him in, doctored his back for saddle sores, got him to movin' an' just now I left him in one of the pens at the livery barn. There was no sign of a rider. We spent yestiddy huntin' an' come up with nothin'."

They went down to look at the animal. Sheriff Walls told the rancher about the mangled dead man. As they were leaning on stringers gazing in at the horse Snowden made a dry remark. "No brand. No identifyin' marks." He paused and with a seasoned stockman's

6

assurance, said, "Seven, eight years old. Up in decent shape he'd be a fine animal."

"Where's the outfit?"

"At the ranch. We'll load it in the wagon next time we come for supplies."

Ben privately agreed that the horse was a breedy type, well put together as he asked another question. "Was there a saddle boot?"

Snowden nodded. "Saddle boot an' a pair of old army saddle-bags. We'll fetch them in too. Nothin' in the bags but some clean pants, a butternut shirt and some soap with a razor. The saddle boot was empty. You expect it's the animal that belonged to your dead man?"

Ben nodded. "Possibly. When are you comin' in with the rig?"

"Next week, for the mail an' supplies. I'll see that you get the bags an' the outfit."

They parted in front of the jailhouse, Sheriff Walls returning to the office with the one barred window, sat down and told himself that without identification the man they had buried with the wooden cross over the mound with 'Unknown' painted on it, must sure as hell have been known to whoever had butchered him.

It bothered him that there had been no shell-belt or holstered pistol, standard attire with folks west of the Missouri River. If he could find someone wearing a sidearm — but how in hell would he know whether it came from the corpse? He couldn't.

It was late summer with autumn in the offing and the advent noticeable with chilly nights. But the days were still warm, occasionally downright hot, and the air was as clear as glass.

When Ellis Snowden's hired hand finally brought in the articles taken off the sore-backed bay horse Ben spent an entire afternoon minutely examining them. He turned up two things of interest. One was a little under-and-over .44 calibre belly gun. The other thing was a scrap of paper, seemingly all that was left of a letter, with the initials W.G. on it.

The local saddle and harness maker, named Walt Gibbons had the same initials. Sheriff Walls visited the harness works where its proprietor drew him off a cup of coffee as Ben asked questions. Gibbons was a greying, youngish-looking person with two dazzling gold teeth in the front of his mouth. He had been doing business in Papago for seven years. Folks knew and liked him. So did Ben Walls but the more questions he asked the less amiability the harness maker showed until he leaned on his counter and said, "What you got in mind, Ben?"

Walls mentioned the scrap of paper and the initials, asked if Gibbons had a friend coming to see him, or perhaps a customer whose name fitted the initials.

Gibbons slowly shook his head. His affability was waning as he said, "You're here because them is my initials," and before the sheriff could speak, he also said, "For your information, Ben, I ain't been up the north stage road in six months an' I got customers who'll tell you that."

Walls finished the coffee, pushed the cup aside and leaned on the counter making a small smile. "It wasn't you. I know that, but all I got is them initials."

Gibbons was not mollified as he shot back a testy reply. "How about Will Garber who rides for Broken Arrow? Or Win Goins? I just finished that saddle in the window for him. Or maybe . . . hell, Ben, you can find a passel of men with them same initials."

That was true. The sheriff left the harness works regretting that he had gone there. He was passing Lacy's sundries store on his way south to the jailhouse when Lewis Lacy intercepted him and asked if Walls had turned up anything about the mutilated stranger, and when Ben shook his head Lacy said, "You know that homesteader north-east of town, the feller named Garrison?"

Ben nodded.

"He's one of them starveout clod-hoppers, never has a second cent to bless himself with. Four, five days ago he come to the store'n bought French toilet water an' some lace-trimmed handkerchiefs for his wife. Things a feller like him's got no business buyin' when he don't even have a sow on that homestead." Lacy paused to make a conspiratorial wink. "He'd been at the emporium too, was wearin' new britches, a new hat and had some other things wrapped in bundles. Tell me somethin' Ben: did that chewed-up dead man have any money on him?"

Walls had understood the implication long before the question. He answered truthfully. "No money on him, Lew, nothin' of any value."

"Not even a pocket watch? Sometimes men got their initials engraved on pocket watches."

"No watch, nothin' I could use to find out who he was."

Lacy, a narrow-faced man with close-spaced shrewd little pale eyes leaned forward and lowered his voice. "Somewhere someone's got his watch."

"If he had one."

"An' maybe his money and other things. If I was you I'd ride out to that homestead. But don't let on I put you up to it."

Sheriff Walls walked the rest of the way to the jailhouse thinking uncharitable thoughts about Lew Lacy, for whom he had never felt much affinity.

Nevertheless the squatter's initials fitted, and for a fact since establishing his homestead Weston Garrison had had to sweep out for Murphy at the saloon and do other odd jobs and with the money he received he bought groceries at Whipple's store.

It wasn't much of a ride, six or seven miles, but as it happened he did not have to ride more than half of it before he saw the gaunt horse pulling the rickety wagon Garrison used when he came to Papago.

They met near a stand of lacy-leaved locust trees. Garrison's wife was a drab slip of a woman with the expression of someone to whom life was a burden. She had freckles over the bridge of her nose and smiled pleasantly when the two men met, but said nothing throughout the exchange between her man and the sheriff.

Walls made the customary banal talk when folks meet; the weather, the lack of rain, the possibility of an early, cold winter, and ended up asking how Wes Garrison was making out on the homestead.

Garrison was a large-boned man, well over six feet tall, who wore a strained expression. Like his wife he was attired in patched clothing. He said things were looking up and although their corn crop had withered and died from lack of rain, they would do better next year.

The sheriff leaned on his saddlehorn. "There's a bank down at Winterton that makes loans," he said mildly and Garrison smiled.

"We'll get by. We bought a sow in town about ready to pig, an' a nice Jersey milk cow. We're on our way to get them."

As the men exchanged a long look Garrison's wife elbowed him. He straightened up. "Sheriff Walls, this here is my wife Bethany. Beth, this here is Sheriff Ben Walls."

Ben solemnly nodded and brushed the brim of his hat. The drab little woman nodded and again elbowed her husband. This time Garrison said, "We'll make it, for a spell now anyway. Beth's ma died back East an' Beth came into some money."

Ben eyed the woman who smiled at him, nodded to Garrison and mumbled something about just riding and lifted his hat as the rickety old rig drawn by the gaunt horse continued on its way.

He rode into locust shade, dismounted

to pee and wagged his head. Lewis Lacy was a gossiping, conniving son of a bitch.

On the ride back to town he rolled and lighted a smoke with the horse plodding homeward on a loose rein.

Clouds were moving in from the east. He considered their soiled edges and thought it was too bad the rain-clouds hadn't appeared a month earlier. A soaking would have saved Garrison's corn. It was close to supper time when he put up his horse, went to the jailhouse, fished in a drawer for a bottle of whiskey and took two jolts.

He crossed to the emporium, found the storekeeper shedding his sleeve protectors which he did every evening at closing time, and asked if the Garrisons had received any mail lately.

What he was told did not raise his spirits. Jared Whipple recalled Beth Garrison receiving a thick letter from some fee-lawyers back East about two weeks earlier. Whipple eyed the sheriff with interest. "Trouble, Ben?"

"No trouble, Jared. See you in the morning."

When the sheriff met Lew Lacy at the café where most of the unmarried men around Papago ate, he nodded, went to sit at the farthest part of the counter from Lacy and listened to a pair of freighters discussing the need for higher rates for the long haul to places like Papago which were miles off the main roadways. One freighter, big, thick and bearded, spoke around a mouthful when he told his friend that anyone hauling freight in northern New Mexico ought to have his head examined. Towns were too few and too far between. He said he was thinking of trailing north into Colorado where the freighting business was better.

Ben arose to spill silver which the half-breed Mex proprietor scooped up as he said, "That feller that got buried some time back? I been tryin' to remember. I think I seen him before."

Ben nodded. "Let me know when

you remember," he said, and crossed through settling dusk to the jailhouse. During his absence either Jared Whipple or his clerk had come over and left mail atop the sheriff's desk.

Mostly, it was Wanted dodgers for outlaws from as distant as Idaho and Texas. He dutifully filed them away. He had yet to encounter a fugitive from those dodgers, but a person could never tell when that might happen.

Up at the rooming-house where single men lived, the sheriff stood briefly at the only window, which faced south down through town, then shed his shell-belt and holstered Colt before preparing to bed down.

It had been a wasted day like every other day when he'd sought answers about the mutilated dead man. Before going to sleep he began the process of withdrawing from any notion he would find the killer — or killers — or identify the corpse. Maybe the 'breed caféman would remember seeing the stranger before and maybe he wouldn't. Also, maybe, since he fed folks from far and wide including passengers passing through on local stages, he only thought he had seen the dead man before. It only occurred to him as he was dropping off that to his knowledge the caféman hadn't seen the dead man. He'd been kept in the ice house until his burial. Not more than a handful of men had seen his face and to Ben Walls's recollection the caféman had not been one of them. He had brought the dead man to town wrapped in canvas and he had been buried the same way.

2

The Storm

ELLIS SNOWDEN came to Papago with the supply wagon, left the driver to give the list to Jared Whipple and crossed to the jailhouse where Sheriff Walls was drawing off his second cup of black java at the little iron stove in a corner. Snowden accepted the offer of coffee, took his cup to a chair, sat down, shoved out his legs, tipped back his hat and said, "You find whoever lost that horse?"

Ben shook his head.

Snowden sipped coffee, blew on it and set the cup aside. "I'll buy that animal," he said. It was customary to auction off ownerless strays, in this case to cover the expenses of burial. The law required impounded animals to be held for ten days before being put up for auction, so Ben said, "I can't sell him for another few days."

Snowden drained the cup, sighed and settled back in the chair looking straight at the sheriff. "We backtracked him as far as we could. He come in the direction of about where that feller you told me about was killed. But — there was two other sets of tracks over-riding the dead man's horse's tracks. Goin' south." Snowden fished in a pocket, produced a spent .44 calibre casing and tossed it atop the sheriff's desk. "We found that thing at the edge of the road in some rocks. If it hadn't been shiny we likely never would have seen it."

Ben picked up the casing, examined it and put it down. It wouldn't be a coincidence that the casing had been found where the mangled corpse had been found, but he had found no immediate trace of the man having been shot and said so. Snowden's response was straightforward. "From what I been told that feller was so gutted, tore up an' mangled if he'd been shot in the soft parts there wouldn't have been no recognizable hole. Did you look for a spent bullet?"

Ben leaned back from the desk. "If you mean did I go diggin' through his guts, which was strung out all over, no, I didn't. But my hunch is that he was shot, which spooked the horse you found."

Snowden nodded thoughtfully, heard someone whistle, nodded and crossed to where his hired man had the wagon loaded and was ready to head home.

Ben went to the window to watch the wagon head north out of town, returned to the desk, sat down and blew out a big breath. He was satisfied in his mind the stranger had been shot. He had over time seen many dead men who had been shot and only once had he encountered one who was still wearing his shell-belt and holster.

He returned to the café for dinner, a tad late, it was almost two o'clock with the sun still high. The café was empty. The dark-skinned proprietor came from behind his curtain, nodded, set a cup of coffee before the sheriff and said, "I been tryin' to remember where I seen that feller."

"Any luck?"

"No."

Ben closed both hands around the cup regarding the caféman as he said, "Gil, when did you see his face?"

The caféman's eyes shifted. "You mean that dead feller?"

"Yes."

"I seen him when I helped Josh Whatly put him in the box."

Ben sipped coffee, sighed and left the café. He had been hopeful. Evidently it was ordained that John Doe was going to remain what had been painted on his headboard, along with the date — 'Unknown'.

Frustration diminished as time passed. Ben's job ensured that other things would occupy him, and they did. If it hadn't been for Ellis Snowden asking questions every time he arrived in town the sheriff would have been satisfied to forget John Doe. The last time the cowman appeared at the jailhouse was when he had made a high bid for the stranger's horse. As far as the sheriff was concerned that pretty well concluded the matter. But Snowden appeared about a week after buying the horse, on horseback this time, not with his supply rig, and he did not look or act as relaxed as on previous visits. In fact he'd barely said good morning when he also said, "Someone stole that bay horse out of our loose stock on the range." To prove he had pondered this he added more. "Ben, there was nine horses had their shoes pulled an' was turned out after bein' used for three months. The bay was the only one missin' when we rode out to see how they was farin'."

"Was he barefoot too?" Sheriff Walls asked, and Snowden nodded. "We yanked his shoes as soon as I got back after buyin' him. He wasn't in no shape to put into the usin' string."

Ben leaned forward on the desk, large hands clasped. "Could you track him?"

Snowden snorted. "Hell no. There's barefoot horse tracks everywhere." He also leaned forward. "He was a good animal, but so were the other ones out with him. Some of 'em was real top workin' horses."

Ben considered the older man. "What you're sayin' is that he was stole maybe by someone who knew him."

"What else does it look like? There's one other thing: there was two sets of shod horse tracks among the barefoot loose stock. Not my riders. We do our own shoein' with plates. Both them other sets of tracks had calk marks."

Ben thought of the local blacksmith as he said, "I'll ask around. If — "

"I already asked Clete. He said he ain't shod a horse needin' calks in months."

Ben was silent a long time. He was beginning to heartily dislike John Doe.

Snowden arose, knocked dust from his hat against one leg, went to the door and turned. "I'll tell you what I think. Whoever that mangled feller was, he wasn't a stranger, someone knew him an' his bay horse. I'd guess someone local."

After the cowman's departure Sheriff Walls continued to sit at his desk. Maybe Ellis was right. For a fact the dead man had been coming to Papago. If he wasn't passing through, why then sure as hell he knew someone in town or in the countryside.

Ben's thoughts were interrupted by Clete Morgan, the blacksmith. Morgan was a wiry man as tough as a boiled owl. He missed being the common conviction that blacksmiths were burly, muscular individuals by a country mile. He sat in the chair Snowden had used and was without his mule-hide shoeing apron. He was a reticent man in his fifties and although he had bought the smithy about six or seven years earlier, all folks knew about him was that he was a crackerjack blacksmith with horses, bowed axles on rigs and even somewhat of a horse doctor.

He mentioned Snowden asking about calk-shod horses and Ben nodded, told Morgan what had happened to the stranger's animal and Morgan shifted a cud from one cheek to the other before commenting. Snowden had already mentioned this to him, and he'd done some ruminating before walking over to the sheriff's office.

He said, "I told Mister Snowden I ain't put calks on a horse in months, and I ain't. But my helper told me after Mister Snowden left that while I was down with croup a couple of days he shod a horse needin' calks. He said he'd never seen the feller before."

"Was that before or after we found that dead man up yonder beside the road?"

"Before, maybe three, four days before."

The blacksmith steadily eyed the sheriff through an interval of silence before Ben asked another question. "Would your helper know the feller if he ever seen him again?"

Morgan shifted his cud again as he nodded. "He said he would. He also said the feller mentioned a friend — that clodhopper north-east of town, Garrison."

"What did he say about Garrison?"

"Only that he sold him a horse once. Knew him around Omaha some years back."

Ben offered coffee, the blacksmith declined and left the jailhouse.

Sheriff Walls kicked back with both arms hooked behind his head. All he knew about the homesteader was that he'd made his claim, had built his shanty as required by homesteading law, and had set up with some chickens, a milk cow, a horse and a woman. Things had gone from bad to worse for Garrison, as it had for many homesteaders from east of the Big Muddy. His personal contact with the homesteader had been limited. It had no reason to be otherwise. Usually, all settled folks had to do was sit back and wait; it took longer with others but eventually they loaded their wagons and left. The territory was marked by dozens of those forlorn abandoned homesteaders' shanties. Cowmen routinely burned them.

The main reason for failure was that while it rained often during hot summers east of the river, west of it, it rarely rained in summer. Homesteaders' crops planted in spring died from lack of rain.

Garrison had been on the verge of being forced to abandon his homestead like the others, until his wife's mother had died. At least that was what the sheriff had been led to believe.

The following morning before sun-up Ben left town riding north-east with no clear idea of why he was doing this. He could not brace Garrison on the strength of what the blacksmith had told him, but he hadn't wanted to sit in the jailhouse doing nothing either.

It was one of those predawn mornings when the air had a heavy scent, there was no wind, and all natural things such as trees seemed to be waiting.

He did not look up until daylight was brightening the easterly horizon. There were thunderheads up there, massive and solidly dark. A raindrop struck the brim of his hat. A slight, bumbling breeze came and went.

The mane and tail of his horse were splaying. He was closer to the homestead than he was to town and as the dollar-sized raindrops began to fall with increasing intensity he reined the horse in the direction of the homestead.

It hadn't been his idea to visit the Garrisons, just to scout the place, but that notion took flight as the raindrops increased to the point that by the time he could make out the house rain was coming like pee through a tin horn.

There was a shed to the left of the house. It had been for the chickens the Garrisons had been forced to eat. He got the horse inside after some coaxing. The animal liked neither the smell nor the darkness but he liked pelting rain less. Ben removed the bridle, draped it from a nail, stood briefly in the deluge before making a run for the house. His knocking was louder than the rain. It required several minutes before Garrison opened the door with one hand behind his back. When he recognized the sheriff he swung the door wide. Inside, because of the heavy rainfall it was hard to be heard if a person spoke normally so Garrison raised his voice as he said, "You're a long way from town, Sheriff. Where's your horse?"

Ben slapped water off his hat as he replied, "In the chicken house." Garrison's drab small woman appeared from behind a curtain which served as a door. She stared without speaking. In poor light Ben couldn't place her expression except that it seemed either worried or frightened.

The homesteader went to a wall

where a shell-belt was hanging, and put the gun he had held behind his back into a worn old holster. As he turned he addressed his wife. "Coffee, Beth. He's soaked to the skin."

Ben was conscious of the puddle he was standing in but Beth Garrison seemed not to have noticed. Her husband seemed almost too affable. He even offered the sheriff a thin sack of Bull Durham which was declined. He said, "We got no whiskey, Mister Walls, which you need right now more'n money." Garrison nodded toward a rickety handmade table with benches. As Ben sat he eyed the small woman working at a wood stove. Even with her back to him she seemed unnaturally preoccupied.

Wes Garrison sat opposite Ben at the table. "You was comin' callin'?" he asked.

Ben was not a very good liar but he tried. "Lookin' for a stray horse. It was dark when I left town. I didn't see the storm until I was close by." Ben cocked

31

his head. Rain atop the roof was very loud. He smiled slightly as he said, "I hope the roof don't leak."

The woman brought two cracked cups full of coffee. She did not look at Ben when she said, "We don't have any sugar. We figured to go to town tomorrow an' lay in supplies."

Ben's reply was both apologetic and grateful. He noticed a small lace handkerchief tucked up one of her sleeves.

Garrison sipped coffee looking at the lawman. "Someone in town lost a horse?"

"No. It was on the range with Ellis Snowden's loose stock. It come up missin' a few days back. Bay horse, he bought it at auction. It belonged to that dead feller from northward up the stage road."

Garrison said he hadn't seen a stray horse and Ben almost replied that it hadn't strayed it had been stolen. Instead he said, "Well, findin' it after this storm will be just about impossible. The kind of rain that's comin' down would wash out the tracks of a thousand-pound bear."

He finished his coffee and cocked his head. Like most thunderstorms this one was passing, the downpour continued but with diminishing impact. As the sheriff arose he grimaced. "They dump too much water for the range to absorb. If I was God I'd sort of thin it out an' keep it comin' for a few days."

Garrison protested at his move toward the door. "You'll get soaked all over again before you reach town."

Ben nodded. The wood stove had about half dried his clothing. He turned toward the drab little frightened woman at the stove. "I'm obliged, ma'am."

She made a slight nod and a smile. "Proud you came by, Mister Walls. We don't often have visitors."

Her husband spoke. "We're sort of out of the way. Last time we had callers was about a month back. One of them travellin' preachers." Garrison smiled. "Somehow they always arrive about meal time."

Sheriff Walls stepped outside, eased the door closed and looked up. There was a watery-looking crescent moon showing through a rip in the cloud cover. The rain was almost down to a light drizzle. He started for the chicken house, halted midway when a blinding flash of lightning startled him. He counted slowly. When the ensuing thunder came he made his estimate, the storm was now sixteen miles away travelling on a north-westerly course.

The second blinding lightning flash occurred as he was reaching for his bridle in the chicken house. It lighted up the shack with bluish brilliance. This time the sheriff did not count, he stared at the floor. There was the clear imprint of a horseshoe with calks. As darkness returned he leaned but it was no longer possible to make out the imprint, but one thing was a surefire cinch, that track wasn't any month old. It wasn't even more than a day or two old and it hadn't been made by his horse, which was plated and never needed calks.

On the ride back he was unmindful of the drizzle. Wes Garrison had lied about visitors. By the time he reached Papago the rain was little more than a damp fog. After caring for his animal he fired up the little iron stove in his office, lighted the overhead lamp and dumped his hat on the desk as he stood with his back to the little stove whose kindling of fat wood had the iron hot in minutes.

Why had Garrison lied and what was his woman afraid of? The storm had done for him what he hadn't evolved a plan to do for of himself. It had provided him with tantalizing questions as well as answers.

The eatery was dark, only Murphy's pleasure palace showed light and because he wasn't much of a drinker after the sheriff was both warm and somewhat dry he locked the jailhouse, hiked up to the rooming-house and was kicking out of his boots when someone rapped sharply on the door.

Ben sighed, stamped back into his boots, opened the door and impassively stared at the weasel-faced proprietor of the sundries store. Ben nodded. "Lew . . ."

Lacy pushed past into the lighted room and faced about as Walls closed the door and remained with his back to it. Lacy said, "I seen you ride past. I looked for you earlier but someone told me you'd rode out before daybreak."

Ben jutted his jaw in the direction of the only chair, went to the bed and sank down upon its edge. He was a patient man, which was fortunate because the sharp-featured storekeeper was one of those people who only came to the point when he had built up the curiosity of listeners. He sat down and smiled. "I got a stranger in the store this mornin' wantin' laudanum and clean cloth."

Ben sat impassively waiting.

"He paid up an' walked out. I watched from the window. He didn't ride down Main Street, he cut through an empty lot and went north up the alley."

"You saw all this from your front window?" Ben asked dryly.

"No. When I seen him cut across them weeds to the alley I went out back an' watched. Sheriff, folks use laudanum to stop pain. They use clean cloth for bandages — wouldn't you say?"

Ben nodded. "Seems likely. Anythin' else about the stranger?"

"Lightning struck as he was passin' my store out back an' clear as day I seen an arrowhead brand on his animal's right shoulder."

"What about the man, Lew?"

"Worn-lookin', like a rangeman. Maybe in his thirties, ain't shaved in days, dark hair, dark eyes, quiet talkin, never smiled."

"You ever seen him before?" the sheriff asked.

"Nope. Never. But I can tell you one thing, under his coat on the left side he had a holstered pistol as well as the one around his middle. Now then — how many rangemen pack a hide-out pistol, Sheriff?"

Ben had to agree, not many. In fact working stockmen rarely even carried belt-guns, they were heavy and awkward if a rangeman had to rope or do much work afoot. They usually wore them on cow-hunting searches in timber country where cougars and bears might be encountered. On those rides they also carried booted Winchesters. Ben asked if the stranger was carrying a saddle gun and Lacy nodded.

Ben asked for further particulars which Lacy could not provide so the sheriff went to the door, held it open and said, "Much obliged."

As Lacy passed to the corridor he turned and said, "After the rain he hadn't ought to be hard to track."

Ben nodded, closed the door and

went back to kick out of his boots for the second time. The rain had stopped but run-off-noise from rooftops continued right up to the moment he fell asleep.

3

The Search

TRACKING the arrowhead horse could wait. The ground would be soft for several days. Ben went down to the smithy where the powerfully built blacksmith's helper, a young man named Abe Tickner, was aligning a tyreless buggy wheel before fitting the tyre. Clete Morgan was not around. The young man straightened up, rubbed both palms down his shoeing apron and said, "Mister Morgan's over at the livery-barn. He'd ought to be back directly."

Sheriff Walls acknowledged this information with an indifferent slight nod as he spoke. "You shod a horse some days back with calked shoes. You remember?"

Tickner remembered. "Stranger,

didn't say much. Sat on that there shoe keg while I put shoes on for him."

"Can you describe him?"

"Well; he was about average height with dark hair, dark eyes an' he hadn't shaved in a spell. Maybe thirty-five, thereabouts."

"Didn't say who he was?"

"No, but he mentioned a friend. No name, just said it the way a man does when he's talkin' about nothin' in particular."

"Was he carryin' a sidearm?"

The massively muscular man nodded. "He had a hideout gun in a holster under his left arm. I seen it when he bent over to spit."

Sheriff Walls said, "Thanks. If you see him again let me know. I'd appreciate it."

After he left the shoeing works Abe Tickner went as far as the wide front opening to follow Ben's progress as far as the jailhouse before returning to work.

Why, Ben asked himself, would this

stranger — and his partner if there were two of them — be hangin' around Papago, particularly if they'd had anything to do with John Doe?

A man could speculate until the cows came home and unless he knew more than the sheriff knew he would wind up with nothing, and in fact Ben had fragmentary scraps, calked horseshoes, loitering strangers, nothing which could not be explained away.

Ellis Snowden walked in during mid afternoon to say one of his riders came on to a horse tied in tree shade near a jumble of big rocks known as Indian Fort and although he searched for the rider he did not find him. Snowden also said, "No one in our country got an arrowhead brand."

Ben asked if the mark was on the right shoulder and Snowden nodded as he made a dry comment. "Horses is usually branded on the left side. Maybe where that animal come from they marked on the right side."

Ben let that pass to ask a question.

"As far as I recollect from ridin' near that field of boulders, there's nothing out there but lizards and snakes."

Snowden nodded again. "When I was a button me'n other kids used to fort up out there like the old-time In'ians. The story my pa told me was that some hostiles holed up in there with the cavalry behind them. He said it wasn't much of a fight, there was somethin' like ten or twelve broncos and two companies of horse soldiers. When I was a kid I looked all around out there for skulls."

"Find any?" Ben asked

"Just one, an' if it was an Indian he must have been really civilized. He had two gold teeth. I took the skull home an' showed it to my pa. He didn't say a word except to tell me to bury the thing." Snowden squinted his eyes nearly closed. "You know what I think, Sheriff? I don't think it was In'ians. I think it was maybe a solitary white man, or maybe two or three, an' I don't think no soldiers run 'em down, I think whites did, an' I think my pa was one of 'em."

"You ever mention this to him?"

Snowden's eyes widened. "Nobody in his right mind ever questioned what my pa said, me included."

Ben understood. His own father had been a man whose word was law, right or wrong. He got the subject back to the rider and his arrowhead horse. "I'll tell you what he looks like, Mister Snowden. Dark hair'n eyes, unshaven, could pass for a rangeman. Carries two hand guns, one like you'n me do, the other one in a holster under his left arm."

Snowden considered that without speaking for a moment. Eventually he said, "What in the hell do you figure this is about, Ben?"

Walls answered candidly. "I got no idea."

"Could this feller be the one who trashed that dead man?"

Again Ben could not answer. "I got no idea."

44

"There's somethin' else, Ben," the older man said. "You know that squatter north-east of town?"

"Wes Garrison?"

"Yes, him. He bought a breedy bay horse off'n a neighbour of mine. You know John Cardiff?"

"Yes."

"That's who he bought the horse from. John come by last week to tell me about the sale. What impressed him was that the clodhopper paid cash off a roll of greenbacks big enough to choke a cow."

Ben's interest strayed. "How far's Cardiff's place from yours, Mister Snowden?"

"A fair distance. I'd say twelve miles or such a matter. He's westerly near where the timber starts an' — "

"How far from them In'ian rocks?"

Snowden paused. "I'd say maybe four, five miles from the Cardiff place. Closer to my yard an' well within the boundary of my northerly range. Why?"

"I'm wonderin' what Garrison was doin' that far from home as the Cardiff place."

Snowden slapped his legs and shot up to his feet. "I got no idea, but for a fact he was that far westerly an' bought that horse off'n John." In the office doorway the cowman faced slowly around. "You know anythin' about that squatter, Sheriff?"

"Very little. Do you?"

"Even less, but now you got me to wonderin'."

When he was alone Sheriff Walls decided to ride out in the vicinity of the Garrison place again. This time he would not leave until after sun-up. His experience with that cloudburst made this decision for him.

It was too late in the day to make the ride. He would do it tomorrow. Clete Morgan was at the café when Ben went over for supper. Clete nodded as the lawman took a place at the counter beside him and did not speak until he'd swallowed. "Abe told me you

46

talked to him this mornin' about that feller he shod the horse for." Morgan leaned back to put a shrewd gaze on the lawman. "Did I ever tell you I was a deputy sheriff over in Idaho for some years?"

Ben looked around in surprise. "You never did. You gave it up to come to New Messico an' buy a smithy?"

"Well, I come here'n bought the smithy but I didn't exactly give up deputyin'. There was an accident on a dark night involvin' a bank. I shot the wrong man, the banker's son. That was years ago. About that dead stranger . . . why would anyone disembowel someone after they shot him?"

"All I know is that we finally found bullet holes in the head," the sheriff replied. "As for the rest of it I got no idea. I never saw anythin' like it before in my life."

The smith emptied his coffee cup before quietly saying, "I have. Do you hunt much, Sheriff?"

"Not much."

"Have you ever seen a carcass after a bear gets through with it?"

Ben ignored the platter the caféman had placed in front of him. Morgan went on in the same quiet voice. "Bears rip. They got claws that slash up meat like knives. I didn't see the bundle you brought back but from what I've heard . . ."

"A bear?"

"They're around out yonder."

Ben said, "Do bears take pistols an' shell-belts?"

Morgan remained unruffled. "Not pistols, but leather that's been sweated into has got salt. Bears are real fond of salt."

"How about the pieces of club-sized wood?" Ben asked.

"Bears chew deadfall wood like dogs chew bones." Morgan arose, put coins next to his empty plate, nodded and got as far as the door before the sheriff called, "Them holes in his head."

The blacksmith nodded. "You ever see what a bear's teeth do to its victims?"

Ben went for a walk with dusk settling. For a fact John Doe had been scattered over several feet of ground. A bear?

He returned to the jailhouse, sat down and leaned far back. There were bears, mostly in high, timbered country but they had also been shot rooting in garbage dumps close to town.

He said, "Son of a bitch!", locked up for the night and went up to the rooming-house.

In the morning he awakened about half ready to believe that was what happened to the mangled stranger, which only complicated things.

He saddled up, with the sun beginning to show and with a spotless sky above. He rode with unsettling thoughts. If a bear had indeed mangled the body, how had it got the stranger off his horse? No man in his right mind allows anything as large and dangerous as a bear to get close to him. Nor does a horse, whose instinctive fear of cougars and bears has to do no more than catch a scent to do one of two things: get the bit in his teeth and run as far and as fast as he can — or, if he's being ridden on slack reins, bogs his head and bucks for all he's worth.

Ben reined to a halt just short of being able to see the Garrison shanty. If the horse bucked off John Doe and John Doe was knocked unconscious from the fall and if there was a foraging bear in the vicinity . . .

"Son of a bitch," the sheriff growled and kneed his horse on a westerly angle which would prevent anyone at the Garrison place from seeing him passing through heavy stands of timber.

It was still chilly by the time he reached one of those infrequent but by no means rare, fields of huge boulders where he dismounted, hobbled the horse and found a place between two horse-high rocks where he could be unseen as he watched the Garrison yard.

If he had arrived earlier, about daybreak, he would have seen Beth

Garrison go to the chicken house where he had stabled his horse during the thunderstorm, but what he did see was when she emerged from the shed carrying a heavy bucket of milk.

He also heard a cow make a plaintive sound because she was hungry.

There was no sign of Wes Garrison. In fact although Ben remained in his hiding place until mid-afternoon he only saw the woman. She came outside once to fling a bucket of water in the direction of some drooping geraniums. The second time she emerged it was to stand under the porch overhang with a hand above her eyes scanning in all directions.

Ben sighed. The woman had been looking for signs of her husband. Worrying females did that. He went back to the horse, removed the hobbles, had his back to the north as he snugged up the cinch when a quiet masculine voice said, "Stand still! Keep facin' the horse! Don't move!"

Ben didn't move. He heard footsteps

approaching. Someone lifted away his holstered Colt and grunted as he flung it as far as he could. For a long moment he was silent but eventually he said, "Are you the lawman from Papago?"

"Yes."

"Why was you spyin' on the Garrison place?"

Ben's hands were near the seat of his saddle. Being disarmed was bad but he'd been in worse situations. He said, "Mind if I turn around?"

"I mind! Don't move, just answer the question. Why was you spyin' on the Garrison place?"

Ben sounded believable when he replied, "I was lookin' for a horse that left Ellis Snowden's loose stock on the range some days back."

"An' you figured Garrison stole it?"

"No. I was out here a few days back. He told me he hadn't seen a stray horse. I come back to hunt on my own."

The unseen man made a grating

chuckle. "So you hid in the rocks watchin' the yard because you figured your lost horse would be down there?"

Ben had never been a successful liar but right now he had to try to be. "Wes Garrison bought a horse off a cowman named John Cardiff fifteen or so miles west."

"What's that got to do with you hidin' in the rocks?"

Ben couldn't provide an answer so he said, "Maybe the horse Wes bought had an arrowhead brand on the right shoulder."

This time the unseen man was silent a long time but eventually he said, "You got a weapon beside the six-gun?"

"No."

"Take off your coat!"

Ben could finally remove his arms from the saddle seat. Behind him a gun was cocked. He dropped the coat and resumed his former position. The gunman had another order to give. "Lean down slow, real slow an' pull up your pants legs."

As Ben stepped back and bent he said, "Mister, I told you. I only had the six-gun."

"Pull 'em up . . . higher . . . right, put 'em down. Lean back on the horse."

Ben obeyed. Before either of them could speak someone down in the vicinity of the shanty raised a high, piping call which was answered by a deeper voice calling back. Ben was facing southward. He saw the rider boost his animal over into a lope and recognized both of them, the woman on the porch who had called first, and her husband atop a fine-boned breedy bay horse.

The gunman said, "Turn around, Sheriff, lead your horse easterly until the rocks give out, then lead it down yonder to the yard."

Ben had done some deducing during this stage of his captivity. The man behind him had been startled by mention of the arrowhead brand, and although there was no mistaking that when he spoke he meant every word, he hadn't sounded sure about what he should do with his captive.

As Ben reached a place where he could lead his animal out of the rocks the man with the gun spoke again. "You're a damn fool. No one with a lick of sense sets where he can't see behind."

Ben could have agreed but he stolidly led the horse in the direction of the yard where Beth Garrison and her husband were talking as Garrison off-saddled. Neither of them looked northward until the horse had been hobbled to graze, then they both saw the approaching men.

Wes said something to his wife. She crossed hurriedly to the house and remained out of sight in there. Garrison stood hip-shot watching the oncoming men with the led horse. He had his thumbs hooked into a shell-belt. Ben became aware of something he had never noticed before. Garrison was left-handed; wore his belt gun on the left side.

When they were close the sheriff's captor raised his voice to say, "Mind him while I go back for my horse."

Garrison barely nodded. He was expressionless as he regarded the lawman. Eventually he blew out a big breath and wagged his head. "What was you doin' that he caught you?"

"Lookin' for that stray horse."

Garrison jutted his jaw. "In them boulders?"

Ben did not reply.

Garrison looked from the lawman's empty holster to his face. "I had a bad feelin' the last time you come out here, durin' that cloud burst. You never come out here before." Garrison's customary diffident affability was gone. In its place was a man with a steady, hard gaze and a quiet menacing tone of voice.

Garrison jerked his head. "Let's go inside, Cliff'll be along."

Inside, Beth Garrison was busy in the cooking area. She kept her back to the

56

men as Garrison pointed to a bench at the homemade table. "Set," he said, and considered the sheriff. "You got a hide-out?"

"No. Your friend went over me up yonder." Ben eased forward at the table considering Garrison. "How much money did your wife inherit?"

"Enough. It's none of your damned business."

"Most likely it's not, but Wes, that breedy horse you got from John Cardiff didn't come cheap. You bought him off a hefty roll of greenbacks."

Garrison regarded Ben Walls in stony silence for a long time before he said, "You're a nosy bastard, ain't you."

"Not exactly, but in country like this the only way to keep folks from knowin' things is to tell it first. Ma'am, if you could spare some coffee I'd be obliged."

Beth Garrison filled a cup at the stove, brought it to the table without once raising her eyes except as she turned away, then she threw a frightened glance in her husband's direction, which he ignored as the door opened and the man Ben had not seen before after his capture walked in, flung his hat aside and shot Garrison a look.

The man Garrison had called Cliff badly needed a shave. His clothing was stained and worn. As Clete's helper at the forge had said, he looked like every other rangeman in the Papago country. His hair was dark and too long. His eyes were also dark. His mouth was a thin wound across the lower part of his face.

As he and the sheriff exchanged a look Cliff addressed Wes Garrison. "Come up behind him. He was settin' between two rocks lookin' down this way. From horse droppings I'd say he'd been up there since mornin'."

Cliff went to the stove, ignored the drab little woman, got a cup of coffee, returned to the table, sat down and gazed at Sheriff Walls through a moment of silence before he half-emptied the cup and pushed it away as he addressed Wes Garrison. "Well?"

"Well what?"

"Him! What do you mean — what! What do we do with him?" Garrison moved to a distant handmade chair and sat down looking at Cliff, ignoring the sheriff who was watching him.

Cliff emptied the cup, shoved it away and twisted to look at Garrison. "I said it before, Wes: you don't have the brains for this business."

Beth Garrison raised her head, cocked it and while drying her hands on a small grey towels said, "He's got to be taken to a doctor!"

4

The Blacksmith Was Right

BEFORE the dark-eyed man could respond there was the sound of a wet moan from behind the curtain which served in place of a door to an adjoining room.

Beth Garrison hastily dried both hands on her apron and passed from sight beyond the curtain. Her husband looked from Cliff to the sheriff. "You know anythin' about doctorin'?" he asked.

Ben heard the sound again and the soft, indistinguishable words of the woman beyond the curtain. Both Garrison and Cliff looked at him. Cliff's expression was disinterested but Garrison's face showed anxiety.

Ben shook his head. "I've doctored horses, a few cattle, but that's all."

Garrison got to his feet, ignored Cliff and jerked his head for the sheriff to follow him.

There were two candles in hurricane casings, one on each side of a handmade bed. There were a table with drawers, a mirror and a bedside table holding a basin of pinkish water.

The man on the bed had been stripped to the waist. Ben stepped from behind Wes Garrison and froze. The man in the bed looked like he'd been through a meat grinder. Beth looked pleadingly at Sheriff Walls. She was holding a bloody wet cloth in both hands.

The man on the bed was not young, amid his awry hair were streaks of grey. His face was dark from exposure but the upper part of his body was white. It had deep gashes over both arms and the chest. The man's gaze at Garrison and the sheriff appeared to lack focus. His lips were grey and chapped. He said, "Cliff?"

Wes answered. "Cliff's out front.

This here is Ben Walls."

"Is he a doctor?" the bloodied man asked and Garrison shook his head. "He's the sheriff."

The injured man seemed to briefly stiffen. When Beth applied the soggy cloth to his forehead he loosened. Garrison spoke to the lawman. "He's Cliff's brother."

"What happened to him?" Ben asked moving closer to the bed.

Garrison replied shortly, "A bear got him."

Ben stood looking down for a long time before leaning to trace out the worst gashes with one finger. Of all the bloody marks there were three that still oozed blood. Ben asked how long he'd been like this. Garrison did not reply, his wife did. "Better'n a week, Mister Walls. If they don't fetch a doctor he's going to die. He gets weaker every day. I've done all I know to do. Those cuts that are bleedin', I can't make 'em stop."

She straightened up and turned. Even

in the poor light Ben could see her expression. He went closer, leaned and made a study of the deepest gashes. What he'd done with horses cut like that was apply powdered blue vitriol to cleanse them and sulphur to make blood coagulate. He asked the woman what medicine she had and her husband answered, "We don't even have no whiskey."

For the first time the woman flared up at her husband in the sheriff's presence. "I told you! He's got to see a doctor. I'll tell you one more time, Wes, if you don't want his death on your conscience you got to get a medical man." She turned to Ben. "Is there a doctor in Papago?"

Ben's reply was delayed. There was a medical doctor. He was very old and frail, about half the time he was out of his mind. Otherwise the nearest doctor was at the army post sixty miles west.

Beth looked down at the injured man shaking her head. "He'd never survive a sixty-mile trip."

Ben agreed in silence, gazed at the mangled man and asked his name. From just inside the curtained doorway Cliff roughly said, "He don't have no name."

Ben ignored the dark-eyed man. "There's someone in Papago who might help him. A woman who delivers babies and patches up hurts."

Beth instantly seized on that. "We got to get her, Wes."

From the doorway Cliff said, "A midwife, for hell's sake?"

Beth turned on him. "He's your brother! What kind of a man are you! He's goin' to die unless he gets help."

Cliff's answer was quietly hard. "We ride into town, get the woman an' ride back? Use your head woman. They already got to know their lawman's missin'."

Beth reached behind to untie her apron which she flung away. "I'll go. Tell her a baby's comin' an' it's not comin' right."

Cliff eyed the man on the bed whose eyes were closed and whose breathing was shallow. Garrison broke the silence. "She can do it," he told the dark-eyed man. "They'd more likely believe her than you or me."

Sheriff Walls said, "Her name's Lisabeth. She's got a little sewin' store north of the livery-barn on the east side." He steadily regarded the man in the doorway. "Maybe she can't help but she's all there is, except for that sixty-mile ride to the army post."

Beth did not await Cliff's assent, she stormed past him, caught up a bonnet on her way outside and kept her back to the shanty's doorway as she caught her husband's breedy big horse, flung the hobbles aside, rigged the animal out, got astride and glared at the two men in the doorway. Her husband made a feeble remark as she reined out of the yard, "You be careful, Beth."

Garrison stood watching his wife ride toward Papago. Cliff turned — and

65

froze. Ben quietly said, "Both of you — shed them pistols. *Now!*"

Garrison stiffened and slowly faced around. He looked from the cocked Colt in the sheriff's fist to Cliff. "You damned fool!"

Cliff glared. "Me?"

"Yes you. Leavin' his shell-belt'n pistol hangin' on the bed post."

Ben gestured with the pistol for them both to get away from the door. Cliff shuffled toward the table looking surly. Garrison went to a bench and sat there. Both their belt-guns were in the doorway.

The sheriff remained to one side of the sick-room curtain. He had the drop but that was all he had. His horse was outside with his outfit. He knew what he should do — take them both to town — but it was a long ride with the afternoon waning. He would be unable to reach Papago before nightfall. He worried less about Garrison than he did about the cold-blooded man called Cliff. Ben was no novice at his trade, he knew exactly how deadly dangerous men like the dark-eyed man were.

Cliff looked at the sheriff and sneered. "Well; fish or cut bait."

Ben's hand holding the gun was sweat slippery. He told Garrison to get some rope, inside the house, not outside. The best Garrison could come up with was a coil of cotton clothesline. Ben told him to tie Cliff's arms behind his back to the chair and moved around to watch this being done. Either Garrison was too upset not to obey or had no compunction about binding Cliff's wrists and upper arms tightly.

Cliff's malevolent gaze never left the sheriff. Garrison returned to his bench also watching the sheriff. Ben said, "Your wife won't get back until late."

Cliff growled, "If she gets back at all."

Ben ignored the dark-eyed man. "We got plenty of time to talk, Wes."

Cliff growled again, "Not a damned word, Wes!"

Ben considered the dark-eyed man. He'd had reason to dislike him when he'd been captured, but subsequent events had turned that dislike into something colder and more deadly. He stepped to Cliff's side, pushed the gun barrel into his neck and said, "Not another word out of you unless I ask for it. Mister, I'd as leave blow your head off as look at you." He accompanied those last words with a savage push of the steel barrel that made Cliff flinch.

Garrison spoke abruptly. "I met Sam — in there on the bed — back at Council Bluffs. We had adjoinin' camps. He come along when we trailed westerly. I never met Cliff until — "

"*Shut up!*" Cliff snarled.

Ben stepped beside the chair again and swung. Steel striking bone sounded loud in the shanty. Cliff and his chair went sideways. Garrison watched the thin trickle of blood work its way through the dark man's hair.

Ben shoved the six-gun into his

waistband, went to the stove where the coffee pot was lukewarm, filled two cups and handed one to Wes Garrison. "He's out of it an' we got lots of time. Start at the beginnin', Wes," he told the homesteader.

Garrison seemed transfixed by the unconscious dark man tied to his chair with a bloody scalp. Wes sipped coffee, got comfortable on a wall bench and watched Wes Garrison who had been confident, even a little cocky, when Cliff had brought in his captive. Right now he looked almost ill.

Ben had patience. He sat, sipped coffee and waited. When Garrison started talking it was like a dam bursting.

"Sam an' me was close friends on the drive west. He said he had a brother up in the Dakotas, at Deadwood. That's when we split off. I heard about them Dakota winters. I come from a place where it snowed six months out of the year. I don't mind a little snow but — "

"Did you'n Sam meet up again?" the sheriff asked.

"About two months ago, him an' his brother an' a feller named Owen Buckley. They called him Buck." Garrison paused to half empty the cup of coffee. "Things was hard for us. Nothin' came right. We had to sell the cow an' eat the layin' hens. I done odd jobs in Papago. Beth said to give it up. We could go back an' I could work for her pa. He owns a saw-mill."

The sheriff put his empty cup aside. "She's a good woman, Wes."

Garrison nodded. "It wasn't none of it her fault. She ain't the quittin' kind but I could see changes. She hasn't laughed in months."

Ben eased the conversation back where he wanted it. "What happened to Sam — what's their last name?"

"Hardin, Sam an' Cliff Hardin. What happened was that Cliff told Sam him'n Owen was comin' down to the Papago country, an' Sam told 'em he knew me

70

down here. So they come, the three of 'em."

Garrison leaned his back against the wall staring at the ceiling. "They come here. Sam saw we wasn't fixed up to board 'em so he rode to Papago and brought back enough to feed an army. Cliff's horse was comin' up lame, it had to have special shoes, so he rode in too. After a few days of just visitin' an' listenin' to me complain about homesteadin', they told me why they'd come down here."

Ben leaned forward, this was the point he'd been waiting to hear.

"An old gaffer up in Deadwood an' Cliff got friendly. Cliff'n the old man got half drunk one night an' the old man told Cliff he knew where there was a cache in minted gold big enough to keep a man in good whiskey an' cigars for the rest of his life."

Ben looked closely at Garrison. He was beginning to tie loose ends together but for the moment he digressed. "Did the Hardins ride for some outfit with an arrowhead brand?"

Garrison made a sour grin. "They stole them arrowhead horses from a trader up there."

With that settled Ben reverted to his hunch. He asked whether Cliff had told him where the cache was and Garrison shook his head. "Cliff's a secretive, devious son of a bitch. All he told me was that he knew where the cache was an' directly we'd go get it." Garrison's gaze slid to the curtain beyond which the injured man groaned. He said, "I wish to hell we had some whiskey."

Ben had another question. "How did the feller yonder get all cut up?"

"We was ridin' toward Papago. Cliff said it was time to find the cache. Just slouching along. Buck said he had to pee so we stopped an' he went off the road among some rocks. Next thing Cliff'n me knew Buck screamed like a wounded eagle an' his horse went past us like he'd been shot out of a cannon. We had a hell of a time keepin' our own animals from boltin'.

It was a gawdamned black bear foragin' in them rocks. Big as a red-back bull.

"When we was able, Cliff held the horses an' I went into the rocks. Mister Garrison, I've seen bears before but this one was not just big, he was a fightin' animal. I shot from the hip. The slug hit a rock. The chips hit the bear in the face. He let go a growl that sounded like a steam train, turned an' run for all he was worth. I shot again. I think I hit him but he never slowed down nor growled. I shot three more times, then Cliff come with his Winchester. But the damned bear was out of range."

Garrison visibly shuddered. "He'd strung Buck all over them rocks. I never seen the like.

"Cliff said we'd go after the bear, which is what we done. But that old boar-bear was waitin'. I guess he was savvy about bein' hunted. We was havin' trouble with the horses. They smelled the bear. While we was fightin' the horses the son of a bitch come out of a tree an' landed square on Sam.

Knocked the horse to its knees. It jumped up an' ran. Cliff shot three times from the saddle. I never got off a shot. My damned horse was buckin' a blue streak."

Garrison paused again. "We brought Sam back here, more dead than alive. I got to tell you, Mister Walls, I never thought Sam'd last this long. What that bear done to him . . ." Garrison leaned far back.

Ben asked if they had found the horse and Garrison shook his head without speaking, and Ben also leaned back. The mystery of the arrowhead horse Ellis Snowden had found and eventually bought was resolved.

Ben asked about the dead man. Garrison said, "Cliff took his pistol, what money he had an' we came back here. I wasn't in no mood to go treasure huntin'. I guess Cliff wasn't neither an' for a fact his brother sure wasn't."

Ben refilled their cups with lukewarm coffee, handed one cup to Garrison and sat down again as he said, "What about the cache?"

Garrison lowered his cup and regarded the sheriff. "What about it? After what we seen over yonder an' after we brought Sam home, I sure as hell wasn't interested."

"How about Cliff?"

Garrison shrugged. "He rode out a day or two later. Didn't say where he was goin' an' I never asked. To tell you the truth, Mister Walls, I was beginnin' to wish they'd never showed up."

Ben had little difficulty fitting pieces together into a kind of rough theory based on what he now knew and what he had wondered about for several days. He asked no further questions about the cache but he had a rough idea of its location. It would have helped if he could have spoken to that old gaffer up in Deadwood but that wasn't even a remote possibility.

Garrison sat gazing at Cliff. "I think you killed him," he said dispassionately. Ben was silent. Probably Cliff Hardin's mother had doted on him as a baby, which would have been before anyone knew what a no-good son of a bitch he was. Garrison's last remark sounded as though he could not have cared less if the dark-eyed man was dead.

But he wasn't.

Ben took the water bucket over and dumped half its contents on the man lying sideways tied to his chair. He sputtered, groaned, and weakly struggled. Ben upended the bucket; when it was empty he put the bucket back near the stove and hoisted the chair with Hardin in it, got it upright and returned to his bench.

They sat like stone watching Cliff come out of his fog. There was drying blood matting his hair and down the front of his shirt. He did not look at the watchers, he muttered, "Whiskey." Neither Garrison nor the sheriff spoke. He slowly turned his head, regarded them through watery eyes which gradually cleared. He said, "Sheriff, I'm goin' to kill you."

Ben nodded. "Not today, Hardin. Most likely no other time either. Wes an' I been talkin'."

A horse whinnied out in the night. Ben went to the door opened it a crack and made out two horses being tied. He recognized Garrison's wife, she was the smaller of two women out there. He spoke without looking around. "They're back."

Garrison came to the doorway, opened it wide for the pair of women to come inside. They both stopped stone-still at the sight of Cliff. The taller woman went directly to him. Ben took her by the arm, steered her to the room behind the curtain and Beth Garrison followed with a candle.

Ben returned to his seat, with one less candle it was difficult to make out details, which did not matter. They listened to the women murmuring in the bedroom and waited.

It was a long wait before the tall woman returned to the larger room looking directly at Ben. She put a little satchel on the table, considered Cliff and without a word went to work examining his torn scalp.

Beth Garrison eventually came back through the curtain. She shot her husband a brief look then went to the stove to put kindling into the fire box to start a fire and placed the speckleware coffee pot above one burner.

Ben watched. Women whose moods or sensibilities had been upset seemed to always go where things were familiar, like their cooking area.

Garrison arose, went to his wife. Her initial reaction was to push him away, then she turned, threw herself against him and cried.

The midwife gave Cliff some laudanum, woodenly asked if she could untie him and when Ben shook his head, she said, "Sheriff, he's got a bad cut. He should lie flat out."

Ben asked a question, "Is he still bleedin'?"

"Not very much, the hair has matted

into a sort of temporary scab."

"Then leave him there."

The tall woman disapproved. Her gaze at Ben Walls wasn't hostile but it was not friendly either. She jerked her head in the direction of the curtain. "Missus Garrison said that one in the bedroom was attacked by a bear."

"Seems likely," Ben responded. "How is he, Lisabeth?"

"Dead, Mister Walls."

5

The Grave

THE following morning because Cliff wasn't up to it Wes Garrison and the sheriff dug the grave. The ground was loam with few rocks but the summer sun was merciless. They sent Beth for water twice before they had the hole deep enough and with squared sides. When they went inside to roll Sam in an old blanket to be carried outside they found his brother had told the midwife to empty his brother's pockets, that he particularly wanted the money and a large gold pocket watch. When she had done these things and was putting what she had found on the table, Wes and Ben walked in.

Cliff asked the midwife to hold the watch up to his ear. "Works fine," he told the tall woman. "I figured that bear might have broke it."

Cliff twisted to regard Garrison and the sheriff. "I got to pee so bad my back teeth is floatin'," he said. When they ignored him, went to the bedroom to roll Sam into the blanket, Cliff spoke from the other room. "Save the blanket. Where he's goin' he won't have to worry about keepin' warm."

They carried the body to the grave, lowered it and wordlessly went to work shovelling dirt. Lisabeth came out, watched in silence until they had the grave half full then she asked a question. "That one inside — were they friends?"

Ben continued shovelling. He neither spoke nor looked at the midwife. Garrison paused to briefly lean on his shovel and answer her. "They was brothers."

The woman stared at Garrison. After a few moments she turned back toward the shanty. Garrison suddenly said, "Where's that pistol he took off Buck?"

Ben stopped shovelling. Wherever it was Cliff hadn't had it when he'd been tied to the chair. Nevertheless Ben dropped the shovel and walked toward the shanty. Too late.

Cliff was waiting over by the stove, the clothesline he'd been tied with lay at the feet of the chair. Beth cowered in a corner. The midwife was sitting on a bench looking about half sick.

When Wes and Ben entered the shanty and saw the empty chair Ben stopped stone still. Cliff said, "I told you, Sheriff, I was goin' to kill you."

The midwife blurted words. "He asked me to at least untie his arms."

Ben ignored her. He and the dark-eyed man looked unblinkingly at each other. The six-gun wasn't cocked but the dark-eyed man had only to raise his thumb to cock it. The distance was too great. Ben went to a bench and sank down. He was sweaty, thirsty and for the moment unable to conjure up any life-saving ideas. Fortunately for him the dark-eyed man was in no hurry, dedicated, malevolent killers rarely were.

Ben tried a ruse. "You shoot that gun an' you'll never find that cache."

Cliff's brows dropped a fraction. "You don't know where it is an' when I leave here won't neither you nor Garrison be alive."

Ben replied quietly. "I know where it is, an' I also know something else. The cowman who bought the arrowhead horse saw you pokin' around in them rocks folks call In'ian Fort the day you tied your arrowhead horse over yonder. And, Mister Hardin, that cowman didn't come down in the last rain, he told me in his pappy's day there was a fight over there. He said he doubted that it was among In'ians an' soldiers like folks believe." Ben paused before continuing. "We talked at the jailhouse after he bought Buckley's horse at auction. I wouldn't bet a plugged *centavo* he an' his riders haven't gone lookin' for your cache."

The dark-eyed man's slightly blood-shot eyes were riveted on Sheriff Walls. His hand holding the six-gun drooped a little. He turned on Wes Garrison. "What'd you tell him, you gutless bastard?"

Garrison could answer honestly. "I said I had no idea where the cache was because you never said. What he just told you is new to me."

The two women were like statues. The tall woman considered Cliff a long time before she spoke; "Mister Hardin, if you shoot the sheriff . . . folks already wonder what happened to him. You kill him and they'll ride you down."

Cliff made a crooked, humourless smile at the midwife. "As far as they'll know, woman, there's a stranger around, because when I leave here there won't be anyone around to say otherwise."

The tall woman, whom Ben did not know well, surprised him now. "Mister Hardin, in my trade you meet all kind of folks. Even some like you."

Ben braced when Cliff cocked the six-gun in her direction. What happened next was totally unexpected. Beth moved timidly toward the stove. When Cliff snarled she spoke in a frightened tone of voice, "I need some coffee. Just one cup."

Cliff jerked his head toward the stove without taking his eyes off Garrison and Sheriff Walls. The explosion was doubly loud because it came from inside the house. Cliff's eyes widened very briefly before he dropped the cocked gun and knocked the table over as he fell.

Ben and Wes Garrison were staring. Beth had been at the stove behind Cliff when she fired. The gun in her fist, which she dropped to put both hands over her mouth, was a nickel-plated .44 calibre under-and-over belly-gun. Its length was no more than five inches.

The midwife stood up, crossed to the sprawled man, knelt to place two fingers on the side of his neck after which she ignored the sheriff and the homesteader to address the drab little woman at the stove. Her voice was crisply professional. "It worked perfectly, Missus Garrison."

Beth went to her husband and crumpled in his arms. The tall woman arose facing Sheriff Walls. Her gaze was direct, steady, emotionless. She said, "I know, Sheriff. You wouldn't have done it. I've never had to use the pistol but I've carried it in my satchel for years. A woman delivering babies in the middle of the night over the countryside has to be ready . . . I told her I'd divert him — gave her the gun and told her to go toward the stove for a cup of coffee."

Ben let go a pent-up breath, stared at the totally calm midwife and eventually wagged his head, arose, picked up the cocked six-gun, considered Cliff briefly and returned to his bench to say, "Wes, you up to diggin' another hole out there? It's hotter'n the hubs of hell."

Garrison was holding his wife whose body shook as she pushed her face into his chest so hard the others could barely hear the sobs.

Wes shook his head.

The tall woman addressed Ben. "I'll help you carry him outside." Then she also said, "If you have no objection I'd like to keep that pocket watch." At Ben's gathering frown she said, "To remember this day."

Ben got the watch and handed it to her. She put it into her little satchel, took Cliff's feet as the sheriff took him by the shoulders and they carried him out of the cabin.

After their departure Wes eased clear of his wife long enough to move a rag rug over two sets of blood on the shanty's floor, one set darkly dry, the other set fresh and red.

Outside, with the sun off-centre but still capable of making heat, the midwife and Ben deposited Cliff near the grave of his brother. The tall woman spoke. "When was the last time you ate, Sheriff?"

Ben considered the woman. If she had a nerve in her body it hadn't showed and did not show now. "Been awhile," he replied.

"Me too. Right now I got no appetite, but I'll cook up somethin' for you if you want."

Ben almost smiled. They were talking about eating over a still-warm body. "Go back to town," he told her and she shook her head. "You go. I'll stay with the Garrisons. They need someone."

Ben couldn't argue with that, certainly Beth Garrison needed someone — a woman.

He looked down. "We better put him in the shade until I can get back."

"Never mind him, Mister Walls. When Garrison is able he and I can plant him." She looked steadily at the sheriff. "You look like hell. I've noticed you many times in town but right now I'd hardly recognize you. Clean up, shave and eat before you return."

She accompanied Ben when he went after his horse, stood in almost stoic silence while he bridled and saddled the animal. When he turned she said,

"Just go. If folks in town ask about me tell them I responded to a call about an overdue baby."

She smiled without humour. "You'll be back tomorrow?"

Ben answered from the saddle. "Right now I expect to, but in my job a man daren't pass his word lightly."

She walked in the direction of the shanty without another word. As Ben reined in the direction of Papago he wagged his head. He had seen her dozens of times, had nodded and had passed along. The almost indifferent idea he had of her was that she was handsome rather than pretty. Otherwise he knew nothing about her except that she was talented at her midwife work and at general attendance of the ill and wounded.

The ride to Papago was long and tiresome, particularly to someone who had missed sleep as well as food for a considerable length of time. His horse walked along on a loose rein. He knew the way, which left his rider free to think back.

He hadn't had any idea of how to avoid being killed by the dark-eyed man and in reflection he thought that what others might have viewed as a miracle was simply the pragmatic, cold-blooded reasoning and planning of a very unusual woman.

It was dark when he entered Papago, for which he was grateful, and after caring for his horse he bypassed the café, which was dark anyway, as well as the saloon, reached the rooming-house, passed down the dingy corridor to the yard out back and filled the none-too-clean zinc bathtub in the wash house for an all-over bath. The water was tepid. The pump sat above a shallow well. Except during the cold months the water usually was tepid.

His back ached, his muscles only very gradually turned loose and he might have fallen asleep in the tub if a foraging raccoon hadn't entered past the ajar door, sat up on its haunches and made a little squeaky grunt. Ben growled and the bandit-faced furry varmint abandoned the wash house in haste.

Ben bedded down and slept like the dead until long past sun-up and might have slept longer if someone hadn't rapped on the door. He called out, "I ain't dressed."

The reply came in a garrulous old woman's words. "You got nothin' I ain't seen before. When did you get back?"

Ben was tugging into his britches when he answered, "Last night."

"Are you decent yet?"

Ben stamped into his boots, ran bent fingers through his mane, sighed and opened the door.

The woman was wrinkled as a prune with little bright eyes like a weasel. She owned the rooming-house. Her husband, dead nine years, had been a soldier who, like many old campaigners, drank. It had eventually killed him.

The old woman considered Sheriff

Walls and pithily said, "When was the last time you seen a razor? Never mind, folks know you're back. Someone seen your horse. I figured I'd ought to warn you there's some cranks complainin' about you being gone so long." The little bright eyes were fixed on the sheriff. "I expect you'll have a good excuse. It just seemed to me I'd ought to warn you."

Ben thanked her, closed the door after she had departed and finished dressing. At the last moment he rubbed his face. It felt like he'd stroked a porcupine so he returned to the bath house to shave. By the time he was ready to show himself the sun was climbing. It was still cool but that condition would not last.

He went first to pitch a flake of hay to his horse and pour an empty coffee tin of rolled barley into the feed box; he then hiked over to the café, which was crowded. At his entrance silence fell. The proprietor showed no expression as he drew off a cup of coffee and placed it at an empty place along the counter. Ben nodded his appreciation and ordered a big steak, fried spuds and two pieces of apple pie.

The caféman retreated behind the curtain to his cooking area. The silence held. Ben ignored the other diners. A cowman arose, trickled coins beside his plate and on his way to the door neither looked at the sheriff nor spoke, but gave him a light slap on the shoulder on his way out.

A late diner entered, saw Ben's back and elbowed his way to the counter beside him. He waited for coffee before saying, "Well . . . ?"

Ben looked around, met the blacksmith's steady gaze and said, "You was right."

"It was a bear?"

"Yes. Feller named Owen Buckley. That bear dropped out of a tree on another one. Feller named Sam Hardin."

At the mention of that name several men along the counter looked up. One of them was Lew Lacy who had the sundries store. "There's dodgers out on the Hardin boys from here to Albuquerque. Rewards out on 'em."

Ben ignored that, ate his breakfast in silence, paid up and departed. The door had scarcely closed when several diners joined Lacy telling what they knew — and thought they knew — about the pair of brothers known as the Hardin boys. Outlaws whose notoriety had spread from Montana to the Mex border. There was speculation too about how much reward money the sheriff would get.

Clete Morgan finished his breakfast, sourly looked around and departed. Across the road the jailhouse door was open. He had left a half-shod horse at the smithy. It would have to wait. He crossed over, nodded and sat down. Ben spoke first, "They're both dead an' buried."

Clete's eyes barely widened. "The Hardin boys?"

"Yes."

"Hard to collect rewards for buried outlaws Sheriff."

Ben nodded. "You know the midwife, Clete?"

"Yes. Knew her husband too. He died three, four years back. Got some kind of complication connected with the summer complaint. What about her?"

"She saved my bacon last night just before dark." The sheriff leaned on his desk with clasped hands gazing at the blacksmith. "I've seen her around but until night before last never talked to her. Never knew her. She's one hell of a woman, Clete."

The blacksmith replied dryly, "I'd say that about a yeller dog if it saved my life."

Walls considered the far wall. "You busy this afternoon?"

"I'm always busy. Why?"

"I got to go back to the Garrison place. I'd like to have you along."

"That string-bean of a homesteader?"

"Yes."

"When do you want to leave?"

"Whenever you're ready."

Morgan stood up. "I left a shoein' job. I'll go tell Abe to finish up, I got business to attend to. Half-hour, Sheriff?"

Ben nodded and continued to sit gazing at the wall after the blacksmith's departure. There hadn't actually been a crime committed. Not in New Mexico anyway, although up in Montana there probably was a horse trader chewing nails and spitting rust over the theft of his arrowhead horses. But that was neither an extradition nor jailhouse offence when the thieves were dead.

Ben went to his little roadway window and looked out. Garrison . . . he had put up the Hardin brothers and the man named Buckley, who was not, at least as far as Ben knew, an outlaw.

Garrison knew who the Hardin brothers were, wanted fugitives from the law, not originally maybe but sure as hell later on.

He thought of the pathetic, drab little woman. As Wes had said she wasn't the quitting kind. Ben returned to the desk and was sitting there when Lew Lacy slid past the door grinning like a Cheshire cat. He sat down as he said, "By my figurin', the Hardins is worth about six, seven hundred dollars."

Ben fixed the lantern-jawed man with a steady gaze. "Get out of here," he said softly.

Lacy's sly smile vanished. He arose and departed. Ben rummaged in a lower drawer for his bottle of 'medicine', swallowed twice and put the whiskey back in the drawer, kicked the door closed and rolled a smoke, his first cigarette in a long time.

The blacksmith appeared out front without his apron and with an old six-shooter strapped around his middle. He was leading a horse he'd got at the livery-barn. Like the proverbial shoemaker whose kids went barefoot, Clete Morgan worked with horses almost every day of his life but did not own one.

He poked his head in the doorway and raised his eyebrows. Ben arose. "Give me ten minutes to saddle up."

Clete returned to the tie-rack. People along the opposite plankwalk stared. The blacksmith was a lifelong addict to Kentucky molasses-cured. He fired an amber stream in the direction of a large bug, missed by inches and watched the bug scuttle away. He never once raised his eyes to the staring people across the way.

When he and the sheriff were riding northward up Main Street neither one of them looked at the staring townsfolk.

Clete waited until they were a mile on their way before speaking.

"You mind tellin' me what happened?"

Ben reacted like an individual who was powerfully glad to talk to someone. He explained, beginning with his capture by Cliff Hardin while he spied on the Garrison place between two big rocks, right down to the moment he would never forget when the little drab, frightened woman had shot Cliff Hardin in the back with the midwife's little under-and-over pistol.

6

Garrison's Bounty

IT was a long ride and no matter how often a man rode it, it got no shorter.

Ben and the blacksmith reached the yard with the sun slanting off westerly. The midwife met them on the porch. Ben nodded without speaking. Lisabeth said, "You shaved." Then she also said. "I buried him. What was in his pockets is on the table. Sheriff, she's a little better but not much. Womenfolk don't often shoot outlaws." At his stare she added a little more. "Mister Garrison told me about the Hardins."

She faced Clete Morgan and nodded. He nodded back and they entered the house. Beth was at the stove and did not immediately turn but her husband greeted the blacksmith and the sheriff

100

with a tired smile.

Beth filled two cups, handed them to the visitors without raising her eyes. She looked haggard. Clete Morgan surprised Ben when he addressed her. "You done right, ma'am. What else could you do?"

Garrison cleared his throat and frowned slightly. Ben and the blacksmith did not mention the Hardins again.

Ben took his coffee to the bench he had used before, sat down and gazed at the homesteader. Garrison seemed to expect what was coming, he stood by the table facing the sheriff when he said, "I know. It ain't over."

Ben tasted the coffee, lowered the cup and spoke quietly. "I got to ask you some questions. It ain't personal."

Garrison nodded.

"First off, you got any of that money left your wife inherited?"

"A little. Buyin' the cow'n horse an' some things for Beth come close to eatin' it up."

The blacksmith went to the stove

to refill his cup. Beth Garrison did not look at him. He returned to a chair, considered the tall woman and sighed.

Ben had another question for the homesteader. "Did either of the Hardins hint around where the cache was?"

"Cliff never, Mister Walls. Sam, he was different from his brother. Him an' me was friends. He told me one night when we was mindin' the horses that Cliff told him he'd asked that old man up in Deadwood why he hadn't gone down here an' dug it up himself. The old man told Cliff he had been ailin' for the past few years, that whiskey was the only medicine that worked, an' he was too old anyway."

"Did Cliff tell his brother where the cache is?"

Wes grimaced. "Cliff Hardin never told anyone anythin'. I expect not even his mother. Sam only knew it was in the Papago country."

"Cliff was goin' to share it with you?"

"That's what he said."

"You believed him?"

"Maybe at first, Mister Walls, but the more I got to know him the more I figured if we found the cache, he'd up an' leave in the night. Mister Walls, as time passed the less I got to likin' Sam's brother." Garrison made a small fluttery gesture with both hands.

"He was here, you see? Him'n Sam an' Buck was here. I daren't try to get rid of 'em."

Beth suddenly faced around from the stove. "Sheriff, all you're doin' is teasing. You come back to arrest me for murder. Do it an' let's get this over with."

Both the lawman and the blacksmith stared at the woman. It was Clete Morgan who sounded indignant when he said, "Arrest you? Lady, there ain't a law court in New Messico that wouldn't give you a medal."

Ben added more. "Ma'am, accordin' to the law murder is when someone deliberately shoots someone who is unarmed an' helpless."

Beth said, "In the back, Sheriff?"

"Ma'am, self-defence means anywhere you shoot 'em. Aback, front or settin' down. You killed Hardin an' saved not just your life but my life an' the life of your husband. I got no reason to arrest you. Like Mister Morgan said, you deserve a medal."

The tall woman went to the stove, took Beth Garrison's hand in her own and led her outside without either speaking to the men or looking at them.

Wes Garrison sank down at the table gazing at the door which Lisabeth had closed behind her. He said, "She didn't sleep last night," and turned to face Ben Walls.

The sheriff rolled and lighted a quirley before returning the homesteader's gaze. He was trickling smoke when he said, "I think I know where that cache is. Somethin' else I think: that old man up in Deadwood most likely wouldn't know where it was unless he was among the fellers who buried it. That happened so long ago I doubt anyone remembers now what was hid or where the loot came from. I expect no one will ever know, but I'll make another guess, gents; that old man had another reason for not comin' back to dig it up. If it was stolen loot an' if he helped hide it, most likely he an' his friends was outlaws, an' old or not, he would be afraid to come back an' dig it up."

Garrison abruptly recalled something. "Cliff once told me'n Sam that old gaffer's name was Kit Wallace. That's all Sam knew."

Ben wasn't interested in the old man's name. He said, "It's a tad late to go ridin' over there now, but if you'n Clete don't mind I'd like to stay here until mornin' an' ride out early. It's a long ride."

The blacksmith, who had been following all this with increasing interest finished checking a sliver of molasses-cured before he said, "I'm willin', if it don't put Mister Garrison out too much."

The homesteader arose. "We'd be proud if you gents'd stay over." He left the shanty to find his wife.

Morgan looked at the sheriff. "What's in that cache, do you know?"

"I got no idea, Clete. It's been out there so long maybe someone else has already found it."

"But you know where it is?"

"Not exactly. I think I know about where it is." The lawman tipped ash off his quirley gazing at the blacksmith. "You got a business to run," he said.

Morgan shifted his cud from one cheek to the other before replying. "It can wait. My helper can take care of things. This won't be the first time he's had to." Clete went to the stove, lifted a burner cover, expectorated into the ash and returned to his chair. "Sheriff, since I was a button I dreamed of findin' a cache. Only in them days it was a pirate's cache. Trouble was, where I grew up we was a thousand miles from the ocean."

Ben stood up. "Better go see to the horses," and led the way outside. Garrison, his wife and the tall woman were standing in the shade of the chicken house, now used as a cow shed. They watched the men leave the house heading for their animals. Garrison told the women he thought the blacksmith and the lawman were leaving. Lisabeth shook her head as she watched the visitors head for their animals and begin to hobble them before arising to remove their outfits. She told Beth she'd go fire up the stove for supper. The drab little woman followed her and Garrison ambled over where the hungry hobbled horses were hopping toward grass.

He brought something from a pocket and held it in his palm as he said. "This was on the table. It come from Cliff's pocket."

Ben and the blacksmith leaned. Morgan said, "Hell, that's obsidian, the stuff In'ians prized real high for arrerheads."

Clete raised his eyes to Garrison's face. "I been in this country quite a while, rode an' drover over most of it. Mister, this ain't black-rock country."

Garrison handed the small stone to the blacksmith. "Maybe Cliff carried it with him from up north. Maybe he carried it for luck."

Morgan turned aside to expectorate before dryly saying, "If that's good luck, may the good Lord never put obsidian in my pockets."

Ben, who had been silently examining the stone, took it from the blacksmith and dropped it into a shirt pocket without saying a word.

The women made a passable meal which, to hungry men, tasted like ambrosia. Beth and her husband exchanged a look. They had been living off whatever he could shoot since eating the last of their chickens. What the men were eating in a thick, peppery grey sauce, was wild rabbit, which was naturally stringy but which hungry men did not object to at all. In fact most folks west of the Missouri River liked tough meat. There had been no other kind for thirty years, not since the last buffalo had been killed.

The women took the only bedroom and although Beth was hesitant the midwife was not and she was tired. They bedded down side by side.

In the other room Garrison handed out old blankets and several quilts. The floor was hard but that too was nothing men like Walls and Morgan hadn't slept on before, and slept soundly.

Before dawn Beth went to the shed to milk the cow leaving the tall woman to work at the cook-stove. When Ben had washed out back and returned he wrinkled his nose and the tall woman said, "You don't have to like it, just eat it."

Beth returned with foamy milk, put the pail aside and took over at the stove. Lisabeth went out back and did not return until the men had eaten. It was chilly outside with only a smidgin of light off in the east. She said she would like to ride with them as far as Papago. They were agreeable.

The last person to leave the house was Wes Garrison, who held his wife close and whispered to her. By the time he came outside the others were ready to ride. They had to wait until he'd rigged out the breedy big horse. Beth stood in the doorway, small, solemn as an owl. She waved as they left the yard with dawn barely breaking.

There wasn't much conversation until they were within sight of the few lighted windows of Papago, then she eased up to ride stirrup with the sheriff, leaned and softly said, "You did right by them, Mister Walls."

He looked around. "My name's Ben an' who did I do right by?"

"The Garrisons," she replied, straightening up in the saddle gazing at the distant lights. "What do you expect to find, Sheriff?"

He grinned slightly. "Somethin' or

nothin'. It seems to me over all the years someone, maybe the fellers who was with that old man who knew about the cache, could have come back. I'd say there's a good chance of that."

She smiled and reined away in the direction of town. "Good luck, Sheriff."

He watched her ride away. Quite a woman.

The blacksmith came up to speak. "You told me on the ride out that ol' Ellis Snowden told you about that In'ian fort, that when he was a kid he found a skull with gold in its teeth. That wouldn't be an In'ian, would it?"

"Not likely, Clete."

"But there was a fight out there."

"That's what Mister Snowden said. I expect if a person asked around there'd be other older folks who would know the story."

"Sheriff, I was thinkin'. If it was much of a fight maybe whoever was makin' their cache got killed off."

Ben looked at his friend. "I thought about that some time back. I thought maybe one feller got clear — that'd be the old gaffer Cliff Hardin knew up in Deadwood."

Clete eased back in the saddle before speaking again. One thing men who were blacksmiths could count on as being as inevitable as death and taxes, was a deteriorating spine. He said, "Sheriff, I got a bad feelin' about this."

Ben nodded. "So do I. We're goin' to ride our butts sore an' come up with nothin'."

"It ain't exactly that," the blacksmith stated and before he could elaborate Wes came up on the sheriff's right side. The sun was brightening the new day from somewhere just below the eastern horizon. Garrison said, "There's somethin' I'd ought to tell you, Sheriff. When Cliff come back from bein' gone all day without sayin' anythin' to me or Sam, his horse was a little gimpy. You got that piece of glass-rock?"

Ben nodded.

"Well, I went out with Cliff to see what ailed the horse an' that's what he had wedged under his shoe close to the quick. Cliff dug it out, looked at it a moment then put it into his pocket."

The blacksmith asked a professional question. "Did the horse favour after that?"

Wes shook his head and commented about something else. "That horse was the only thing Cliff showed any feelin' for. He kept him shod with calked shoes. He said it eased the strain on his tendons."

This time the blacksmith nodded without speaking.

Ben told the homesteader as far as the law was concerned Garrison could claim both the Hardin brothers' horses on a claim against them for feed.

They had been riding westerly and a tad northerly. As the world steadily brightened they could see the jumble of age-old rocks called Indian Fort. They were on Ellis Snowden's range and had been for several hours, and while they saw bands of cattle freshly out of their beds and grazing, they did not see any other living creatures.

Clete wondered aloud if they hadn't ought to go by the Snowden place and tell the cowman what they were about. Ben had thought of that and had ignored it. Ellis Snowden wouldn't care, particularly this time of year when cattlemen would be driving cattle to their farthest ranges which would be grazed off first, after which the cattle would be gradually drifted closer to the home place until, during winter, the cattle would be close by, easy to keep an eye on, and grazing over feed saved for winter.

The last half-mile the men rode in silence studying the jumble of large rocks which covered close to an acre. No trees grew in the boulder field. There were tall weeds, patches of grass, otherwise just rocks, some tall enough to hide a horse.

When they halted to dismount the

blacksmith said, "How in tarnation did it come that them rocks is all in this one place with no other rocks anywhere around?"

He got no reply. Ben led the way into the field of rocks, in places having to use one hand to avoid twisting an ankle or getting a boot caught between boulders. Clete made another observation. "Nice place. Rattlesnakes sure as hell. Sheriff, a man'd have to be awful hard-up to come into a place like this."

Again, the blacksmith got no reply.

The sun was not quite as high as it would be in another hour or so, which by then it would be directly overhead.

The blacksmith sat on a rock considering his surroundings. As he did this the sheriff scuffed among rocks, picked up something, went over where the blacksmith was sitting and held out his hand. Morgan said, "Glass-rock for a damned fact," and stood up.

Wes also looked at the shard in the

lawman's hand, but he said nothing, just straightened back looking around, after which he finally spoke. "A man could poke around in here until the cows come home."

Ben pocketed the scrap of obsidian and gestured for Garrison to search to the north, for the blacksmith to search to the south and began a careful advance westerly.

He was conscious of one disadvantage. If there was indeed a cache here, after forty or more years mother nature would have pretty well scabbed over any signs of it such as digging.

Ben had progressed a fair distance, eyes watching the ground, when he thought he heard a horse blow its nose. The sound came from the west. They had hobbled their animals on the east side of the boulder field.

He paused, thought it must be either Ellis Snowden or one of his riders and resumed his foot-by-foot search.

The heat increased. It did not help that they were in a field of rocks which just naturally absorbed sunlight and flung it back.

Ben was nearing the westerly limit of the boulder field when he heard rocks being flung aside. The rattle of this noise was unmistakable.

He halted, listened, decided the noise was coming from the north and somewhere behind him. He sat on a rock to closely examine the boulder field to the north and also to the east. The noise stopped, then was resumed. He fixed its location in his mind, arose and began a careful stalk in that direction.

Most of the rocks were too small to shield a man but not all were. Ben's stalk included moving from one tall boulder to another. He had to cross places where he would not be concealed but there was nothing he could do about that.

The noise stopped, silence settled and Ben paused to lift his hat, mop off sweat and reset the hat, brim tugged low to shield his eyes.

He patiently waited for the noise to be resumed but it wasn't so he stealthily resumed his way and got a surprise he would never have imagined.

There was a small area, no more than ten or twelve feet around where rocks had been cleared away. In the centre of it was a woman, old, stringy, with long grey braids who was attired in patched trousers, a butternut workman's shirt which was too large, and nearby leaning against a boulder was a Winchester saddlegun.

The old woman had a shell-belt around her middle with an old hawgleg Colt in the holster. She was sitting back on her heels squinting westerly. She did not move. From Ben's vantage point she did not even seem to be breathing. He wondered if she had heard someone, perhaps Wes Garrison who was hunting northward.

Very gradually she turned in Ben's direction, squint-eyed and expressionless, claw-like old hands on her upper legs, for all the world like an ancient squaw except that she clearly was not Indian.

Ben was about to move into her sight when a quiet voice spoke from behind him. "Don't move, mister. Lift out the gun an' let it drop."

Ben involuntarily stiffened. This made the second time someone had got the drop on him from behind. He emptied the holster and turned very slowly.

7

The Strangers

"**I** TOLD you I heard someone," the old woman said, arising to face the sheriff. "And who might you be?" she asked. Before answering Ben slowly turned. The man holding the pistol was as sinewy as the woman but younger. He had pale eyes, a weathered set of features and gave the sheriff look for look. His six-gun was cocked.

Ben introduced himself. "Sheriff Ben Walls from Papago."

If either the old woman or the man with the gun were impressed neither showed it. The old woman used a wrinkled cuff to wipe sweat off her forehead. Her eyes were as pale as the eyes of the man with the gun. She said, "How come you to be prowlin' in this rock field, Sheriff? Lookin' for outlaws, was you? Well, let me tell you, sonny, you're better'n forty years too late."

Ben eyed a flattish boulder and asked if he could sit down. The old woman nodded. "You lookin' for somethin' are you — what'd you say your name was?"

The man with the gun sounded exasperated when he said, "He said his name is Ben Walls."

The old woman ignored the man with the gun. "Mister Sheriff Walls, what are you doin' out here in the heat of the day?"

Ben had ample time to make guesses about the old woman and her companion. He answered quietly. "Most likely the same thing you're doin' out here," and gestured toward the small rock-free clearing. "Is that where you figure it's hid?"

The man retrieved Ben's gun, shucked out the loads and handed it to Ben. The old woman stepped into some thin, meagre shade before speaking again.

"What makes you figure anythin's hid here, Mister Sheriff Wells?"

"Walls," the man with the gun said. "W-a-l-l-s."

The old woman gave the man with the gun a venomous look before returning her attention to the sheriff. "He's my son. Don't pay him no mind. He thinks he knows it all. Answer me, Mister Sheriff Walls, what makes you think there's anythin' hid here?"

Ben had no doubt that eventually Wes and Clete would hear talking so he was slow, almost ponderous, in his replies, but truthful.

"The story come down here from Deadwood. An old man up there told another feller. Him an' two others come down here to find the cache."

"Where are the other two?" the old woman asked sharply.

"Dead. There was three all told an' they're all dead."

The woman's eyes narrowed on the sheriff. "You killed 'em?"

"No ma'am. A bear got one. The

other two just had bad luck."

The woman gave a bird-like nod of her head. "Who told 'em the cache was here?"

"Some old man up in Deadwood named Kit something or other."

The old woman stiffened, shot her companion a look then said, "You remember the last name, Mister Sheriff Walls? By any chance was it Wallace?"

Ben nodded and the old woman and her companion exchanged another look before the woman said, "That lyin', miserable, son of a bitchin', renegade horsethief an' worse. He was my husband an' Justin there is his son. We thought he was dead."

Ben said, "By now he may be for all I know. The feller he told about the cache said he was older'n dirt an' ailing."

The old woman wasn't finished with her recriminations. "He left me with a baby, the rat-tailed bastard. Over thirty years back he saddled up to meet some friends, and never come back."

"Who were the friends, ma'am?"

"I don't know."

"If he deserted you how come you to know about the cache?"

"I knew it was somewhere in these rocks because he'd used it before. Once after a stage robbery, another time after he plundered a bank. He told me he'd hid enough loot in old Snowden's rock field for us to live easy for the rest of our lives."

Ben considered the angry old woman. "If he said that to you why would he run out on you?"

"The last time he raided a store down near the border. That time they come within an ace of catchin' him. He got home with a hole clean through the calf of his leg. I nursed him like a mother — the no-good son of a bitch — set up night'n day, run an' fetched until he could walk . . . got up one mornin' an' the bastardly old screwt an' his horse was gone. Deadwood, did you say? For a plugged cartwheel I'd go up there an' shoot him!"

The pale-eyed man leathered his gun, sought shade, sat on a rock and gazed at his mother. "We been all over this a hunnert times," he said dryly. "He's been out of our lives since I was in diapers. Like we done ever since, forget him an' let's get on with it." He faced the sheriff. "Where do you think the cache is?"

Ben answered candidly. "Somewhere in this field of rocks. That's all I know, an' it might not be there, either. Unless your pa was the only one who survived a shoot-out, then it might be, but if someone else got free, I'd be willin' to bet you a good horse it ain't."

The old woman addressed her son sharply. "We gone over this a hunnert times. Justin, your pa got clear an' no one else did."

Justin looked at Ben. "What all do you know about the cache?"

"Just that it's supposed to be in these rocks."

"How much loot is in it, Sheriff?"

"I just told you, all I know is

that it's supposed to be in these damned rocks." Ben gazed at the shiny cartridges nearby and leaned to pick them up. Neither the old woman nor her son interfered. He put the bullets in a pocket and asked the woman a question. "Mind tellin' me your name, ma'am?"

Her son answered. "Fanny Wallace. We come a hell of a distance — from down near a two-bit place called Peralta."

Ben watched a scorpion cross his boot and scurry on its way. It hadn't raised its tail where the poisonous stinger was, which meant it hadn't been fearful. He smiled crookedly at Justin Wallace. "Quite a happenstance, you arrivin' here the day we did."

The old woman picked up on that one word. "We? You ain't alone?"

"No ma'am, an' if we set here long enough they'll come along."

"Lawmen like you, Mister Sheriff Wells?"

Justin dropped his head and shook

it. "Walls, Ma, gawddammit can't you ever — ?"

"Shet your mouth! You nag at me one more time . . . Justin, you got some of your pa's bad ways in you."

If Justin might have defended himself he did not get the chance. The old woman glared at Ben. "How many friends you got out here, an' don't lie to me."

Ben gazed dispassionately at the old woman as he replied. "I got no reason to lie to you, ma'am. Two other fellers, a homesteader an' a blacksmith."

"Deputized are they?"

"No. No reason. As far as I'm concerned there's been no crime committed."

Clete Morgan's twangy voice said, "Not yet. You there settin' on the rock, toss the gun away. Old woman, don't touch that saddlegun."

The blacksmith did not appear until Justin had disarmed himself. The old woman glared daggers but made no move toward her Winchester.

Clete came from behind rocks gun in hand. He did not take his eyes off the Wallaces as he spoke to the sheriff. "I crouched down an' listened. That's the first I know that old screwt up in Deadwood was an outlaw."

Ben leaned and shoved his legs out. "It was obvious, Clete." The blacksmith gestured with the Colt in his fist in the direction of the old woman's clearing. "Is that where it's hid?" he asked. Ben did not answer the question, he asked one of his own. "Where's Garrison?"

"I got no idea," the blacksmith replied, squinting at the place which had been cleared of rocks.

Ben arose to look northward and easterly. If the homesteader had been where he was supposed to have been, by now he would have heard talking. Ben sat down. Gone, he told himself. Half-way back to the shanty by now. If Ben went back there the shack would be empty sure as hell was hot.

The old woman startled him out of his reverie. She had been squinting at

Clete. She said, "What do you do for a livin'?"

Clete was as startled as the sheriff. "I'm the blacksmith over at Papago."

"What's your name, mister blacksmith?"

"Clete Morgan."

"Mister Morgan, you married?"

"No ma'am. Never got around to it."

"Who does your cookin' an' all?"

Morgan holstered his six-gun and sank down on a rock. "I eat at the café an' sometimes hire my washin' an' such like done."

Fanny Wallace spared a glance for her son, who was staring at the scuffed toes of his boots when his mother again addressed the blacksmith. "I'm a widow, sort of, Mister Morgan, a good cook an' done tons of washin' an' such like. That there's my son, Justin. Justin shake hands with Mister Morgan."

As the handshake was performed Ben saw the look on the blacksmith's face and stifled a smile.

Fanny Wallace spoke again, her pale gaze fixed on the blacksmith. "When we find the cache, Mister Morgan, there'd ought to be plenty to go around. If you'n me — "

Justin interrupted. "Ma, for hell's sake — "

"Shet up, Justin! Mister Morgan . . . "

Clete was on his feet as he ignored the woman and addressed the sheriff. "I'm dryer'n a bone. Let's get this over with." He turned in the direction of the little clearing and without looking at the old woman asked her why she had been searching in that particular place.

If she'd been a snake she couldn't have hissed her brusque reply any better. "Because that's where I went with Justin's pa, the no-good, lyin', robbin' son of a bitch, to bury the loot from a store robbery." She twisted to glare at the bare place. "Someplace . . . I know I'm right."

Ben dryly asked a question. "How long ago was it you came here with

130

your husband, ma'am?"

She understood the implication and glared. "You think I'm addled or maybe forgot the place? Let me tell you, Mister Sheriff Walls. I remember things from thirty years back better'n I remember what I had for supper last night. Somewhere right around here is the cache!"

Ben was in shade, sitting comfortably. He eyed the old woman as he asked another question. "Why did you wait all them years before comin' here?"

"Not that it's any of your danged business but I had a child to raise an' a livin' to scratch out sellin' eggs in town, washin' dishes at the eatery an' all. I didn't have a second cent to rub against the first one, an' comin' this far north would cost more'n I had, right up until Justin got to drivin' freight. Then we had enough money." Her glare was unrelenting. "Now you answer a question for me, Mister Sheriff Walls."

Both Ben and Clete involuntary braced and Justin stared hard at the scuffed toes of his boots.

"Do you'n your friend figure to get the loot? Because if you do, let me tell you I'll shoot you both if you try!"

Justin raised his head. "Ma, for all we know there ain't no loot, an' these fellers — "

"Shet up, Justin. Don't you take sides with no lawman'n a blacksmith against your ma."

Justin didn't shut up. He said, "It's hot out here. If all we're goin' to do is talk I'd as leave ride off, Ma." Justin stood up. "I'm thirsty. The horses'll be shrunk up like gutted snow birds. Are we goin' to go on with this jawbonin' or are we going to find the damned cache?"

Before Fanny Wallace could speak Clete said, "Lady, it'll be sundown directly an' I'm dryer'n a bone. You can spit or close the window as far as I'm concerned. Are we goin' to look for the damned cache or not?"

The old woman saw the identical expression of total disgust among all

132

three men. She wiped sweat off, shoved one grey braid off her shoulder and said, "You bring diggin' tools did you?"

Ben shook his head.

She spat words at him. "What 'd you expect? Just walk in here, push some rocks away and get rich?" She turned before Ben could reply. "Come along, an' you mister blacksmith, you mind your manners. If there's one thing Justin can do, it's draw faster'n shoot straighter'n anyone you ever seen."

There was no shade at the cleared place, the sun was off-centre on its westward course but the heat would not diminish for hours. Fanny Wallace halted and pointed toward some rocks she had flung aside. "That's it. Somewhere, I'd have swore it was under them rocks."

Justin dryly murmured. "But it wasn't."

The old woman ignored her son. "I swear to Gawd this is the place."

Ben twisted to glance around. It all

looked pretty much the same to him, small, round, dark rocks with only occasionally larger rocks, some much larger.

Thirst was a problem. It awed the sheriff and the blacksmith that the old woman seemed impervious to both heat and thirst. Ben thought the reason had to be that she believed herself to be close to the loot.

The men half-heartedly kicked some rocks aside, flung some away and with a widening perimeter worked at this without speaking or looking at one another. Ben's mood was sombre. He hadn't expected instant success but neither had he anticipated what had happened since he arrived at the so-called Indian Fort.

Clete paused to fling off sweat and scowl at the sheriff. "Where's the clodhopper?" he asked, and Ben dryly answered, "Most likely pretty close to bein' back home by now."

Clete scowled. "After we come this far, this close? What'd he run for, he didn't commit no crime?"

Ben had no answer so he offered none.

Justin suddenly swore and recoiled. The others didn't hear the rattling sound until Justin picked up a rock and heaved it. He must have missed because the rattlesnake increased the sound it made.

Fanny called to her son. "Don't shoot, Justin. Lord knows who else is sneakin' around out here."

Justin moved farther back and picked up another stone; when he turned to hurl it the snake had disappeared. Clete said, "Don't touch no more rocks, kick 'em."

It was valid advice but neither that particular poisonous snake nor any others were encountered.

The sheriff abruptly halted. At his feet the small rocks were all around as it appeared they probably had been since the beginning of time.

Clete called to him. "Ben? What is it?"

Instead of answering Ben kicked some rocks aside, leaned and picked up a skull. The others stood like statues as he examined it and finally offered it to the blacksmith who also examined it before raising his eyes to say, "Shot in the back of the head."

They gathered to study the skull. Ben looked for gold teeth but there were none. He kicked other rocks aside, gleaned an area of about ten feet before he leaned a second time to pick something up, this time a badly rusted, weather-deteriorated gun. He tried to open the loading chute looking for ammunition but it was frozen in place. He raised the old weapon to catch sunlight in the cylinder. As he lowered it he said, "Well, I guess that explains about the feller shot from behind. The gun wasn't fired."

They left the old gun atop a stone and continued their search as the sun continued to sink and there was no let-up to the heat. Once, when the old woman, using a long stick to poke and pry, came close the sheriff asked her where their horses were. She gestured westward with the stick and resumed her poking and prying without saying a word.

The old woman's son abruptly quit and sought shade. His mother ignored him and everyone else as she poked and pried. The only time she even hesitated was when perspiration ran into her eyes, then she used a soiled cuff to rid herself of the annoyance.

It was her son, sitting morosely watching the others who suddenly raised an arm as he said, "There! Right about where the sheriff's standin', that big cracked rock."

Ben identified the cracked rock and turned. "What about it?"

"The crack, dammit. There ain't no other rocks been split. Look around."

He was correct, of the dozens of rocks large and small the boulder he had gestured toward was the only one that had been cracked. The split was about six inches wide.

The old woman came over to shield her eyes with one hand and squint. Clete approached the boulder, ran a hand inside the crack and jerked it out with an exclamation. Following the hand was a large scorpion and this one had his tail curled high to strike.

Justin laughed. No one else did. The old woman used her stick with satisfactory results. Although the scorpion repeatedly struck the stick she killed it. It fell at Ben's feet. He instinctively back pedalled.

Justin came over tugging on a pair of rider's gloves. His mother said, "Mind what you're doin'. Don't stick your hand in there."

She might as well have spoken to the cracked boulder, her son groped for the edge of the split, gingerly groped down inside it, continued to grope with the others watching, leaned back to extract his gloved fist. When he opened the fingers he had another old rusted firearm, this one with ivory grips and two initials scratched into them. K.W.

The old woman took the gun, held it close then began to sweat, "He told me he lost it after the store robbery, the lyin' bastard." She looked up. "What was it doin' in that rock?"

Ben made a guess. "He put it down in there so's he'd know exactly where the cache was."

They considered the boulder; even if they moved it, and it broke apart during the process, the boulder weighed easily six or seven hundred pounds.

Clete shook his head. "A mule couldn't budge that thing."

Ben studied the ground as he replied. "Dig, Clete. Dig under it. Dig deep enough then get behind and push like hell."

The old woman offered an admonition none of them needed. "Don't be in front when it rolls."

Ben dropped to his knees. Fortunately the summer-hard ground was shot through with ancient rock chips which made it easier for men without tools to scrape dirt away.

The old woman watched and finally said, "You goin' to dig to China? Justin, get away from there, that thing's fixin' to roll."

She was right but the big rock did not move until the men all got behind and heaved at the same time. The old woman, a good thirty feet away, squawked like a chicken and ran.

8

The Odd Rock

IT was a good thing that the old woman ran because the boulder sagged drunkenly as it tumbled into the dug-out place, broke completely in two and both halves rolled in the direction the old woman had run, not far but far enough; if she hadn't run she would have been squashed.

Dust arose, two large wood rats half as large as house cats flung up out of the ground where the boulder had sat and fled, large rocks were not supposed to move, especially ones that had been in place for maybe 10,000 years. One rat ran directly toward Clete, who aimed a wild kick and missed.

Before the dust settled Sheriff Walls batted it away and approached the place where the boulder had been. He stopped dead still.

Clete came up, stared and softly said, "I'll be gawddamned."

The old woman came back, and with her son stood like the others, staring.

There were a number of leather pouches and something wrapped in what had once been a horseman's poncho but what held the sheriff's attention was a small wooden box which was being prevented from disintegration by four steel corners and a massive steel hasp. The wood, though, was punky rotten.

Ben went forward, dropped to one knee and forced the little box open. Inside were more little leather pouches. Some had disintegrated and gold coin lay scattered. He rocked back on his heels as Clete unrolled what was left of someone's riding coat. Inside were what appeared to be hastily hidden personal belongings. Three ruined old six-shooters, a saddlegun, three sets of spurs and what could have been *chaparejos*, called chaps in many places. These were the shotgun variety which riders pulled on over their trousers in thorny country, not the modified version used by northerly rangemen who worked countries where there was no thorn-pin or cactus and which were fastened behind the leg with either small thongs or metal snaps.

All had been chewed to bits by varmints.

The old woman was gathering those little doeskin pouches like her life depended on it. Several broke the moment she lifted. Money fell out and an occasional piece of jewelry which Justin identified as being of Mexican origin, and he should know, he had grown up far enough south to know articles from Mexico.

The old woman withdrew from the others with her little pouches, squatted and opened each pouch one after another. She had the contents in a neat small pile. She ignored everything and everyone. She had more silver and gold coins than she had seen before in her life.

The men ignored heat and thirst. By the sheriff's estimate the cache contained no less than $5,000 in coin. Of paper money, which had been rolled and tightly bound with thongs, there was probably more than $5,000, but varmints, probably wood rats, had eaten some notes, had used others for nesting material, and the notes which had not been vandalized by critters, nearly a half century of rain had made into coloured paste.

Clete fondled the paper rolls almost wistfully until Ben handed him two pouches from the steel-reinforced box.

Justin knelt near the sheriff. He reached into the box and Ben struck his hand away. Faster than anyone saw Justin drew and aimed at the sheriff. His face was taut and sweaty. His mother called to him. "Put it up, boy! You hear me? Put that damned gun up!"

Justin obeyed but with obvious reluctance. He and Ben exchanged a long look before Ben spoke. "Yeah, I know. You'n your ma been waitin' a lifetime for pay day. You'll get your share."

Clete had discarded the pouches and put the coins in his pockets. He said. "Six hunnert dollars, Sheriff. Divvy it up."

Justin watched Ben like an eagle as the sheriff began gathering the loot and sorting through it. The varmint-chewed rolls of bank notes he tossed aside and Justin gathered them up. He mother came over to stand behind the sheriff looking over his shoulder. When he had the loot evenly divided he twisted to ask how much she had taken. She spat her reply. "It's mine. By Gawd it's less'n half what I got comin', an' no one's goin' to take it from me, Mister Sheriff Walls."

Justin looked from his wild-eyed mother to Ben and said, "Nine hunnert dollars. I watched her countin' it."

The old woman would have berated her son if the sheriff hadn't said, "Keep it, ma'am. You're right about havin' it comin'."

Ben concluded the division. The smallest stack of coins remained in front of him. Clete raised his eyebrows and Ben shrugged. "By rights I just come over here for the ride."

He stood up and rolled a smoke. The old woman's claw-like fist came out of nowhere. She held a sputtering sulphur match for the lawman. He thanked her and smiled. She didn't smile back. If she had her prune-like old face might have cracked. Fanny Wallace had not genuinely smiled in thirty years.

Each person's share of the loot including jewelry and salvageable paper notes was more than any of the men could have made working for wages in five years.

The old woman gruffly told her son it was time for them to go. In fact with dusk on the way it was time for all of them to go.

Clete's bothersome thirst seemed to have been thoroughly compensated for by the weight of coins in his pockets. He turned once as he and Ben were picking their way easterly to look back. There was no sign of the old woman and her son, too many huge rocks hid them.

The horses were in bad shape. With more surface area they suffered more from lack of water than people did.

Clete made an unnecessary observation as he removed the hobbles. "You're right, Sheriff, Garrison quit."

Ben's reply was dry. "It could be worse, Clete. He could have turned our animals loose an' set us afoot."

As they were heading south-westerly the blacksmith said, "The damned idiot."

Ben replied dispassionately, "You never know when a man's guts will give out. I'll guess the reason he run back was because of his woman."

Clete's brows shot up. "She didn't have nothin' to do with it."

"No, but we left her alone an' them three graves'd be out there every time she went for water at the well or went to milk the cow. I think she's as tough an' loyal as Garrison said, but everybody's got a breakin' point. I figure her husband knew that."

"But hell, another few hours an' he'd have been able to go back to her with real money."

Ben let the topic drop.

The sun was gone and while the heat had lessened it did not become cool until the lights of Papago were distantly in sight.

By the time they reached the west-side alley in town the scent of water had encouraged their animals to come up in the bit.

Ben left the blacksmith riding south toward the livery-barn and off-saddled his own horse in its corral. He had to make it slack off at the trough several times and stayed with it until the danger of founder was past, then he pitched it feed, dumped the coffee tin of rolled barley in the feed box and entered the dark jailhouse from out back. He lighted the hanging lamp which needed cleaning but gave off enough light, went to the desk, tossed his hat aside, sat down and felt dampness on the front of his shirt where he had tanked up at the trough with the horse, leaned back, put the small stack of cache-money on the desk and blew out a big sigh.

Papago was lively as it usually was about supper time and afterwards when the menfolks gathered at Murphy's watering hole.

He fell asleep in the chair. When he awakened Papago was quiet, even the saloon was dark. He stood up and flinched. His feet were swollen inside his boots. He went to douse the light when someone rattled the roadway door. He gruffly called out, "Go away."

The knock came again, not loud and not insistent, but nevertheless persistent. He opened the door wearing a menacing scowl. It could have been Lacy from the sundries store but it wasn't.

The tall midwife had a light *rebozo* over her shoulders, except for that Ben wouldn't have known he had slept most of the night away.

He stood aside for her to enter, returned to his desk and sat down. The tall woman put a folded slip of paper on the desk. He made no move to touch it. She said, "You'll sleep better, Sheriff."

He unfolded the note. The handwriting was neat and small with wide spaces between the words. He read it, reread it and looked up. The tall woman said, "I rode out there. She was bundling things. She said her husband told her before he left with you he'd be back as soon as you got so far off you couldn't catch him." The tall woman paused. "You look worn out. I'll come back tomorrow."

He shook his head and pointed to the nearest chair. She sat down. In the poor light she looked ten years younger. In that same light she did not look hard, capable of getting a man shot.

Ben gazed at the note, which was a sad and lonely woman's expression of gratitude. It mentioned nothing about leaving. He leaned back off the desk. Lisabeth arose. "Tomorrow," she murmured and was going toward the door when Ben stopped her. He pointed to the little stack of coins as he said, "We found it."

She hesitated. "So I see."

"Set down," he told her and she dutifully returned to the chair. He gazed at her in the smoky light. "He didn't have to leave."

She contradicted him. "Yes he did. She would have left without him. She's not the homesteading kind, not in this kind of country."

"Will they go back East?"

"Yes. Wes can work for her pa. He owns a saw-mill."

Ben already knew that. "If he'd waited another few hours he'd have shared in the loot."

She cocked her head slightly at him. "Let me ask you a question, Sheriff."

"Ben."

" . . . Ben; let me ask you a question.

If you had to choose between a woman you loved or money, which would you choose?"

He reached inside his shirt to scratch. That was a hard question to answer for a man who had never been married or particularly attached to a woman.

She spoke again when it seemed he was not going to. "I don't know why, but you've been missing the greatest experience a person ever runs across."

He looked at her. "The woman, I suppose."

She gathered the shawl around her shoulders which he correctly interpreted to indicate she was going to leave, so he said, "There was an old woman an' her son already out there. Her husband was the feller up in Deadwood who told Cliff Hardin about the cache. The old feller was an outlaw named Kit Wallace. Him an' some friends hid their loot in that boulder field on the Snowden place." Ben paused to gently wag his head. "That old woman was meaner'n a snake an' tougher'n rawhide." Ben almost smiled. "The old man up in Deadwood run out on her thirty some years ago, leavin' her with a baby. Ma'am, that old woman could make a man's hair stand up when she was mad — which was most of the time."

"What became of her?" the tall woman asked.

Ben leaned forward with clasped hands. "They left, that's all I know. She had about half the loot. Between her'n Justin, her son, they got enough to set easy for a long time."

"You thought she deserved it?"

Ben nodded.

This time when the tall woman arose and went to the door Ben did not stop her. She turned with a small smile and said, "Tomorrow, Ben. Goodnight."

As a matter of fact it was a good night. So good Ben didn't awaken until the smell of cooking aroused him when the sun was well above the far curve of the world.

News of his return to Papago had spread. Only God knew how, except that 'moccasin telegraph' among locals was faster, although as a rule not as accurate as telegraph.

When he appeared bathed and shaved at the café it was later than most of the caféman's regulars ate, but there were still a few. One of them was weasel-faced Lew Lacy. When Ben walked in the silence was thick enough to cut with a knife. The dark caféman smiled, filled a cup with coffee and put it at the counter. Ben nodded his gratitude and ordered enough breakfast to choke a horse. Still no one addressed him, but eventually Lacy had to. He said, "There's talk around about you'n the midwife."

Ben turned. "You son of a bitch!"

Lacy left and a grizzled cowman shook his head as he said, "His ma would have done better to have pinched his head off an' raised calves on the milk."

No one addressed the sheriff. He finished breakfast, shoved the plate away and pulled in a refilled cup of coffee. After the last diner had departed Ben asked the caféman a question. "You ever feed a scrawny old woman an' a younger feller sort of wore-down lookin'? Their name was Wallace."

The caféman shook his head. He would have remembered; very few women patronized his eatery.

Ben crossed over to the jailhouse. During his absence someone from the general store, which also served as Papago's post office, had placed several letters on his desk.

He was opening the first letter when Clete Morgan walked in. He too had scrubbed and shaved. He sat down and smiled, the expression resembled the look of the cat who ate the canary.

He said, "If I live to be a hunnert I'll never forget yestiddy." Ben nodded.

"Do you know what happened to the squatter?"

Ben handed Morgan the note. As the blacksmith read he pursed his lips and, as he tossed the letter back, he said,

"One more gone. The cowmen'll burn the shack some night. Well, the world's full of folks who don't know their butts from a round rock. He missed out on sharin' an' for that I got to say he's a damned fool."

Ben tapped Beth Garrison's note. "I know you never been married, Clete, an' I know that old woman liked to scairt the whey out of you yesterday, but someone said to me last night that when the choice is between a good woman an' money, a man'd do best to pick the woman. His wife was goin' to leave with or without him."

The blacksmith listened to all this and shoved up out of the chair. "You ever considered bein' married, Sheriff?"

"No."

"Me neither. Maybe we're missin' somethin'."

Ben said, "Maybe," and watched the blacksmith depart after which he re-read Beth Garrison's note one more time and leaned with both hands clasped behind his head staring into space right up until Josh Whatly and the harness-maker Walt Gibbons walked in looking and acting breathless. Walt blurted out sentences that ran together.

"There's been a shootin' south of town a piece; the northbound stage come on to it an' brought one of the fellers to town all shot up. The other two fellers is dead, he left 'em out there."

Ben got to his feet. "Where is he?"

"At the midwife's place," the harness-maker said, less agitated than the town handyman but excited nonetheless. "He don't look like he'll make it, Sheriff."

Ben herded them out, closed the door after himself and walked briskly in the direction of the tall woman's cottage, which was on the same side of Main Street as the jailhouse but farther south, down near the livery-barn.

The blacksmith saw him passing in a fast walk and went to the shop's doorway to call over to the sheriff. "Somethin' wrong?"

Ben called back. "Down at Lisabeth's place. There's been a shootin'."

Clete stood still with his jaw sagging as he watched the sheriff turn in past the sagging gate of the midwife's place. He came to life with a shout to his helper. "Abe! I'll be back directly." He flung his apron aside and crossed the roadway in front of a pair of rangemen he did not see. One started to remonstrate but his companion said something and both riders continued on their way toward the edge of town.

Down there the annoyed one said, "Damned fool didn't even look. I'd have run over the top of him."

The second rangeman looked back but there was no sign of the blacksmith. As he settled forward he said, "That was Clete Morgan, the blacksmith. That's the fastest I ever seen him move. It must've been somethin' real important."

His companion was not mollified. "I saw who it was. His eyesight must be failin', the danged old fool. Walked right in front of me no more'n five feet from the horse's nose."

The other rangeman changed the subject and a mile farther along when their animals were 'warmed out' they boosted them over into the rangemen's favourite gait, a rocking-chair lope.

Lisabeth admitted the sheriff, saw the blacksmith coming and left the door open. She did not say a word as she led Ben to a small bedroom in the back of the house. Ben was shocked, not entirely by the basin of bloody water on a little table, nor the mound of discarded blood-stained cloths on the floor beside the bed, but rather by the wide-eyed stare of the pale-eyed man. It was Justin Wallace!

Lisabeth said, "They brought him in an hour or so ago. He comes and goes. Do you know him?"

Ben leaned to examine the bandage which was being soaked through. Lisabeth brushed his arm and pointed. "The bullet went in there and came out in back on the right side. I'm sure there's internal bleeding." She paused to rinse and dry her hands. "If it don't stop on its own I don't know what to do. I'm not what he needs — a medical doctor."

"He's Justin Wallace. I mentioned him last night. Where's his mother?"

"All I know is that they told me there was a gunfight somewhere down the south stage road. Two got killed and this one they brought back."

"Remember me tellin' you last night about an old woman an' her son?"

"Yes. This is her son?"

Ben nodded as Clete appeared in the doorway. The sheriff turned toward the blacksmith. "Hire a horse. Maybe the old woman's down yonder somewhere."

As they were leaving town southward Clete asked and Ben told him what he'd been told, and that was all he said for four miles, until they came to a place a stager had applied his binders so hard there were five-inch deep skid marks made by steel tyres in roadway dust.

9

The Unexpected

THERE were tracks, two went north in the direction of Papago, another set went south-easterly. Ben jerked his head for Clete to follow as he paralleled the single horse tracks. The blacksmith said nothing but he hadn't come down in the last rain either; the pair of horses running toward town swerved back and forth the way riderless horses do. The single set of tracks never deviated.

Clete was frowning when he said, "Three of 'em, Sheriff. You see them dead ones back yonder? They never knew what hit 'em. Right through the brisket both times."

Ben rode in silence. The old woman had told him her son was deadly with a six-gun.

There should have been another set of tracks. Justin and his mother had ridden two, the killers had ridden three.

Clete came up with the answer. Neither of them had heeded tracks in the roadway. It wouldn't have told them anything if they had. The road had tracks by the dozen, not only of wheeled vehicles but of saddle horses, shod and barefoot.

Ben squinted ahead where the tracks skirted around a long groundswell. Clete frowned. "If he's around there we're settin' ducks."

Ben scanned the skyline of the landswell, saw nothing which might have been a watcher and reined northward. It was a long mile but when they reached the terminus where the landswell slanted toward flat country they rode around it. Ben's assumption, prudent and thoughtful, was that if the fleeing rider saw them coming he would be waiting at the southerly end of the landswell because he would know they were tracking him.

What occurred was unexpected. They saw the grazing, riderless saddled animal before it saw them. In fact they were able to approach within a quarter of a mile before the saddled animal raised its head and froze.

Ben said, "Well now, he's around here someplace."

Clete agreed while studying the sidehill south of them with its inevitable growth of rank underbrush. "An' when we're in range . . . "

Ben halted within roping distance of the saddled but riderless horse. "Don't make sense," he said, both hands resting on the saddlehorn.

Clete's reply was crisp. "Yes it does. Look south along the slope. That's where they was hid. There are the signs of hobbled horses."

Ben shifted his attention as the riderless horse dropped its head to resume cropping grass. The three men had been watching the road from behind the landswell for some time. Horse droppings told him that much.

Something else caught his attention, two sets of tracks showed clearly heading due east. He said, "They set up an ambush. After the gunfight one man come back here." He pointed. "Two riders ran for it."

Clete leaned studying the ground near the lower slope of the hill. He expectorated. "There must have been four, Sheriff."

Ben nodded. "Maybe, an' maybe the one who come back here was ridin' double. Clete, two horses run north. Most likely they belonged to those dead fellers back by the road. The feller who survived come back here where there was a hobbled horse."

"On foot from the road, Sheriff?"

"No. On the old lady's horse, ridin' double with her because sure as hell it was Justin's horse that run toward town, an' if they'd shot her we'd have found the body by now."

Clete scratched his head. All this figuring was confusing him. He shook out his reins and started riding eastward parallel to the new sets of tracks. Just once did he comment and that was when they were a mile and more on the new trail. "Why would he burden himself with the old woman?"

Ben had no idea. "Maybe he can tell us when we find him. I'll tell you one thing: at the rate they're goin' in this heat there's not a horse on earth who can keep it up for long."

Clete was still trying to follow the sheriff's convoluted thinking when Ben raised a stiff arm. In the distance there was a faint banner of dust and nothing else, no trees, no big rocks, just cow-country grassland.

As he lowered the arm Ben said, "They're slackin' off."

Clete wasn't convinced but he rode in silence for as long as was required for him to make an estimate of the time which had passed between Justin's arrival in Papago and the pursuit by himself and the sheriff. Eventually he said, "They should be farther off than that dust."

Ben rode in silence. Maybe the blacksmith was right but the tracks led directly in the direction of the dust banner. Clete was right but the sun was high before they made that discovery. They found the old woman. She was sitting on the ground in the middle of nowhere when they eventually rode up and halted.

She looked up at them from an expressionless face showing where tears had run down her cheeks. Ben dismounted, handed Clete his reins and went to sink to one knee beside the old woman.

She turned slowly as she said, "They killed Justin."

Ben gently shook his head. "He's alive. The midwife in Papago's carin' for him. What happened?"

The far-away look did not diminish as Fanny Wallace slowly put words together. "We seen 'em comin'. They raised their right arms friendly like. When they was close to the road one of 'em fired at Justin. He went off his horse. It run off. I got down as Justin fired twice. He emptied two saddles. The other one got down an' swung his horse so's he was behind it. Justin toppled over. I went to him. He was hit hard, bleedin' bad an' didn't open his eyes. I grabbed his gun but when I turned this feller was right behind me with his cocked six-gun pointin' into my face. He told me to drop it an' I did. He looked at Justin, said he was dead an' for me to get behind the saddle with him."

Ben interrupted. "He didn't rob you?"

"He was scairt peeless. All he figured on was gettin' away from the road as fast as he could usin' me as a shield. We rode hell for leather for a landswell, behind it was a hobbled horse. He hit me alongside the head, told me to get on one of them animals an' stay up with him. It's been many years since I've rode bareback but I stayed with him until the horse stepped in a hole an' I fell off. He never even looked back. The loose horse run off with its tail over its back."

Clete dismounted. "There was a saddled horse behind the landswell, ma'am."

She nodded. "Did you look at the saddle? There was blood on it. They caught a preacher the day before, robbed him, hauled his carcass into some brush and took his animal. The feller who carried me along didn't offer to let me ride the preacher's horse, but when we was a-horseback and I quarrelled with him about ridin' bareback, he said the preacher's horse had a ringbone and was limpin' when they bushwhacked the preacher beside the road."

Ben raised his eyes to consider the easterly countryside. There was no movement and no dust. He lowered his gaze. "Who were they?"

"I never seen 'em before. They was highwaymen. Murderin' sons of bitches," the old woman said, and held out a hand. "Help me up."

Ben got her upright and asked another question. "Did they get your loot from the cache?"

The old woman gave the sheriff an annoyed look. "I told you. They sure as hell didn't expect Justin to be good with his pistol. After he killed them two the scairt one wasn't thinkin' of anythin' except to get as far off as fast as he could. No, they didn't get time to rob me."

The old woman eyed the townsmen. "My boy ain't dead?" she asked.

"Not when we left town," Ben told her. He refrained from mentioning that between the three of them, Ben, Lisabeth and Clete, they did not share even a small hope that Justin would be alive when they got back to Papago.

Clete went to his horse, snugged up the cinch, got astride and held out an arm for the old woman to get up behind the cantle. She protested. "You can't overtake that murderin' bastard with me slowin' you down."

Clete gazed dispassionately at the

woman. "The nearest settlement from where you're standin' ma'am, is sixty miles. You got no horse, no water . . . quit your danged arguin' an' get up here."

She accepted the outstretched arm, swung up, settled behind the blacksmith and they resumed their ride, but this time without any of their earlier haste.

It was hot, the sun was slanting away but that meant only very belated relief from heat.

Ben rode ahead paralleling the fleeing man's tracks. He did not say a word until the sun had sunk noticeably lower, then what he said was addressed to Clete. "You know the Clavenger place?"

Clete shook his head so the sheriff raised his arm pointing slightly northward. "About ten miles. They'll have water."

Clete said nothing. The tracks hadn't deviated, they were still heading easterly as straight as an arrow. In his opinion even a slight deviation would allow the fugitive to widen an already considerable gap between pursued and pursuers. He also worried about Fanny Wallace. He might have worried more if she hadn't raised one hand to his shoulder and said, "Mister Morgan, Justin's a good boy. I'll be lost without him."

Clete's answer was careful and wary. "He'll pull through."

"You're plumb sure, are you, Mister Morgan?"

Clete swatted at a deer fly before answering. "If he's as tough as his ma, he'll do just fine."

Ben altered course a little. Clete leaned looking for tracks.

They too were changing course. Not much but noticeably.

After another couple of miles Ben looked around to say, "I got a bad feelin', Clete. He's sashayin' more north-easterly."

"You figure that's bad?" the black-smith asked.

"Toward the Clavenger outfit."

"His critter's got to need water too, Ben. If there's folks up there I hope they hold the son of a bitch."

Ben lifted his hat, mopped off sweat, lowered the hat and rode slightly to one side watching the tracks. Once, he looked up at the position of the sun, then looked down again. By his guess they were within five or six miles of the Clavenger yard. It would help if dusk came early, which of course it would not do; horsemen in this flat grazing country stood out like a sore thumb. Movement was what folks watched for in flatland country, and movement under a bright sun was recognizable for one hell of a distance.

Clete was thinking the same way otherwise he wouldn't have said, "Not a damned tree, not even a hill. Ben, we could set out here until sundown." Even as he said this he knew what the reply would be and it was.

"We're not stalkin' him, Clete, we're goin' to ride him down."

Clete spoke softly aside to the old

172

woman behind his cantle. "Whatever you do, ma'am, don't ride with Ben Walls when he's chasin' someone."

The old woman's reply had nothing to do with the blacksmith's suggestion. "My name is Fanny, not ma'am."

Clete tried to inch forward a little but his saddle had only a thirteen-inch seat. He scrooched as much as he could which was not enough, Fanny Wallace's hand still rested on his shoulder and her breath was still on the back of his neck.

An old cow with six-foot horns came out of a gully so suddenly the horses both set up hard and fast. The startled riders did not see the young wolf streaking through tall grass until the cow bawled and increased her rush to the limit. It was a dog wolf no more than two years old and it was running for its life. If it saw the stationary riders it showed no signs of it. It was stretching so far its belly guard hairs were brushing the ground.

The old woman said, "He's old

enough to know better'n to tackle a full-grown cow."

Clete spat aside before replying, "The way she come up out of that gully, she'll have a calf down there."

The cow ran out of wind but the young wolf kept running until he was lost to sight. The cow saw the riders, ducked her head, pawed and rattled her horns. She was drenched with sweat, her tongue lolled and her eyes were glazed.

Ben led the way a quarter-mile out and around the old girl who watched, head high and tail switching. The last they saw of her was when she wheeled and disappeared back down into the arroyo.

Fanny Wallace made an odd remark. "Females'll fight quicker'n males to protect their young."

Neither Ben nor Clete had anything to say about that.

When they got back to the fleeing man's tracks they could make out an assortment of buildings in heat-hazed distance. It was afternoon but still, it was one of those days a man on horseback seemed to ride forever toward buildings, towns, even mountains that stealthily retreated before him.

Clete asked if the sheriff knew the folks up ahead. Ben's reply was cryptic. "They trade up at Benchmark. It's closer'n Papago. I've met 'em a few times. The old man's one of them old In'ian fighters, hard as nails. His wife's pretty much like him. They got a son. If I remember right his name's Aaron. That's about all I know except that they been ranchin' out here since the mountains was holes in the ground."

What worried the blacksmith as well as the sheriff was that the tracks they were dogging went arrow-straight in the direction of the Clavenger yard. Clete was squinting toward the buildings when he said, "Those folks ever been in trouble with the law, Ben?"

The sheriff was also watching the

buildings when he answered, "Not that I know of. Not that I ever heard."

Clete said no more but the old woman did. "I'm beginnin' to have a bad feelin', gents."

They all were as they came within a mile of the buildings and a distant dog began to bark.

They could make out two men emerge from a huge old log barn and a woman come out on to the porch of the house. Clete had another question. "They got hired riders, do they?"

Ben had no knowledge of that either, except that any cow outfit this time of year that ran a thousand head or more had riders. All he said was, "Likely", as he watched one of the men duck back into the log barn and the other one hike toward the house with long strides.

The dog had short hair and a sort of mottled hide. It was one of those dogs that threatened at one end and wagged its tail at the other. Ben rode past it into the yard as his horse cocked its head slightly, ready to kick if the dog tried to nip it, but the dog stood well aside so the men from Papago and their passenger rode up to the log barn, dismounted, looped reins at the rack and were turning toward the house when a rawboned big old man, grey as a badger, stringy as rawhide emerged. He had a six-gun on his right hip with a shell-belt from which about half the loads were missing.

He did not smile, stood with his head cocked slightly back as he came to the far side of the rack, looked longest at the old woman before saying, "Evenin', folks. I'm Carl Clavenger."

He shoved out an oversized, work-roughened hand which Ben briefly gripped as he introduced himself, Clete and Fanny Wallace.

The rawboned old man stared hard at Fanny. She returned his stare look for look. Eventually he said, "Ma'am, there's wash-water at the house. That's my wife on the porch. Her name's Abigail. Folks call her Abbie."

Fanny Wallace neither moved nor showed gratitude for the extended welcome. She said, "There's outlaw tracks leadin' here, mister. Right up to the edge of your yard. This here is Sheriff Walls of Papago County. Where is the son of a bitch that come here?"

Clavenger's eyes widened a little as he regarded Fanny Wallace. Profane womenfolk were not exactly commonplace. He faced Ben to speak.

"How close did them tracks come to the yard, Sheriff?"

"Couple hundred yards, give or take. It looked to us like he was comin' here. We been trackin' him since mornin'. Him an' some other fellers murdered a preacher an' shot Missus Wallace's boy. They tried a highway ambush. Her son put two of 'em down to stay. One of 'em shot him. He's bein' taken care of in Papago. Mister Clavenger — "

A man called from the porch. He had a saddle-gun in both hands. Clavenger addressed the sheriff before acknowledging his son's yell. "We

178

been bothered lately, Sheriff, an' we're pretty much on our own this far from neighbours an' all. My boy's real leery."

Clavenger returned the shout from the man on the porch. "It's Sheriff Walls from Papago."

The younger man, the spitting image of his father in height and build came across from the house still holding the Winchester. He, Ben and Clete shook hands. The younger Clavenger did as his father had done, he stared at Fanny Wallace. She reacted typically.

"Well, boy, I ain't here by choice!"

They moved to the shade of the porch as a lean, short man came through the barn from out back to lead the animals to water first, then down the runway to be unsaddled and cared for.

Carl Clavenger's woman was of the same stock as Fanny Wallace. She was taller and heavier but the slant of jaw, the closed hard set of the lips and the steady eyes were the same. She took

Fanny inside after the introductions, and came back a little later with a pitcher of spring water and cups for the men sitting in porch shade.

Ben began with the failed highway robbers and ended up relating where they had last seen the tracks south of the Clavenger yard.

The old man dropped his hat beside the chair, vigorously scratched a grey thatch and looked at his son. "Maybe," he said, "that's what Shep was barkin' about." He faced Ben Walls. "We come out an' looked around but saw nothin'. Figured it was maybe a digger squirrel or maybe a coyote. The dog even barks at low-flyin' birds." The old man squinted out across the sun-bright big yard a moment before speaking again. "You sure the tracks come close to the yard? Maybe you got side-tracked. Maybe you was followin' the tracks of one of our riders."

Ben scotched that. "Any of your riders come in the last few hours, Mister Clavenger?"

The old man shook his head. "They're miles off, won't even get close until sundown." The old man squinted against sunshine and spoke to the sheriff without looking around. "Why would a feller like that come here?"

Ben improvised an answer. "His kind, the kind he rode with, ain't above attackin' isolated cow outfits. I've known 'em to stay hid out an' watch a place like this for days."

"Only one man?" Clavenger's son asked, and Ben nodded.

Clete, who had been silent up to now said, "Water an' a fresh horse."

10

A Long Ride

THE short man who had taken care of the visitors' horses came briskly hiking from the direction of the barn. He had a noticeable crabbed stride. Before he was within hearing Clavenger softly said, "We sort of inherited him. He was born with a crooked leg an' ain't right in the head."

The crippled man's eyes were wide as he stopped at the steps and said, "There's a beat-down horse out back of the corral."

All the seated men followed the short man to the barn, down through and saw the horse trying to get its head through corral stringers to the water trough. Clavenger said, "Get him inside," to the crippled man. "Don't let him drink more'n two or three swallows then get him away. He's been rode danged near to death."

Clete and Ben exchanged a look. The sweaty foam showed where a saddle had been. Along the side of the animal's head were signs where a bridle had been.

Aaron Clavenger spoke aside to his father, who faced the men from Papago. "I expect we know what he come for, gents." He turned to the short man whose mouth hung open. "Jimminy, did you see a man down here?"

The short man ran a grimy cuff over his mouth before answering. "I seen him, yes sir. He come in from the far side."

"Did he get a horse, Jimminy?"

"He got a horse. That long-legged roan Aaron rides. Saddled him right outside the gate and rode that way." The short man raised an arm to indicate northward.

Clete and the sheriff squinted northward. There wasn't a sign of movement. No movement, no dust. Clavenger only briefly looked in the way the man who had stolen one of his animals had ridden. He spoke to his son. "Saddle us a couple of animals, Aaron. Sheriff, we'll mount you on fresh animals. Yours is wore down."

The rawboned old man also said, "That horse-stealin' son of a bitch. You got to give him credit, Sheriff. Right while we was settin' on the porch."

Abigail Clavenger appeared on the porch hands folded beneath her apron, stony-faced, still and silent. Beside her Fanny Wallace also watched the men leave the yard. She said, "I hope they lynch the son of a bitch."

The larger woman looked down. "First they got to catch him. Come along, we didn't finish the tea."

The sun was canting away. In the distance the land gradually changed from grassland open country to lifts and rises, trees and rocks. One place they passed Clavenger pointed. "See that bosque of oaks, Sheriff? There was an Arapaho rancheria there when me'n my pa come here. Friendlies; we give 'em a beef now an' then. Good In'ians." Clavenger looked ahead where the country got rougher. "Army come one mornin' ahead of sunrise, surrounded the camp and give 'em ten minutes to come out unarmed. I was pretty young. My pa told the captain the In'ians caused no harm, they was friendlies. When the time was up the In'ians lined up without weapons an' the army drove 'em south like we drive cattle. They never come back."

Ben studied the large older man. Nothing seemed to upset him. They were after a horsethief and Carl Clavenger mentioned something that had happened maybe fifty years earlier.

Tracking was easy until they got into rocky country where oaks, both black and white oaks, grew in large clumps. Here, Clavenger rode slightly in the lead. His son told Clete Morgan his pa could read sign over a glass window.

Evidently it was the truth. Clavenger halted once with both hands resting atop the saddle horn. When the sheriff came up Clavenger raised his arm. "He's cut back south-westerly. Sheriff, you reckon he knows this country?"

Ben had no idea. "All I know is that he rides hard an' fast. Why?"

"Well, south-west there's an old abandoned homestead."

"Does it have water?"

"Water an' the house's got adobe walls four feet thick. Messican made it. He starved out twenty years ago. That'd be the only water, Sheriff. If he'd kept northward he'd have come to a sweetwater creek. That's why I asked. I'd say he don't know the north country but most likely he knows where that old mud house'n water is."

Ben addressed the cowman. "Suppose we cut straight for that place instead of followin' his sign."

Clavenger nodded slightly. "I was thinkin' of the same thing. I can tell you from experience, gents, trackin' someone — you're always behind him."

They changed course and picked up the gait a little for a couple of miles. Where they dropped back to a slogging walk Aaron Clavenger addressed his father. "I'll go ahead." His father said, "You'll stay with us." Aaron stayed.

To the north that broken country with its bosques of trees was on their right. The country they traversed after changing course had trees, but not in bunches and the land was typical flat grassland.

The sun was in their faces when Carl Clavenger drew rein where six or eight gnarled trees cast shade. He dismounted without speaking until the others had also gotten down, then he raised an arm. "No more'n two, three miles," he said, and lowered the arm. "He'd see us comin'. We can rest here until dusk."

Clete spoke quietly to the sheriff. "An' suppose he ain't at this place up ahead? We'll lose him sure as grass is green."

Ben waited until the horses had been hobbled, the men lying comfortably using saddle-seats for pillows before he went to Clavenger with Clete's thoughts.

The rawboned old cowman's answer was slowly given. "Directly I'll scout afoot, but it's got to be darker'n it is now. If he ain't there we can still make good time after dark by anglin' back northward until we find his tracks. Set down, Sheriff. We'll get him."

Clavenger left the trees when dusk was settling. The others sat, talked a little and waited. When he returned he said, "Well, he's been there. Plenty of sign, but he left headin' south."

As they left the resting place Clete told Ben if that cowman could read all that off the ground in the dark he must have owl's eyes.

Clavenger led his horse. There was a two-thirds moon but the going was slow. Too slow for the blacksmith until Ben told him they at least had someone along who knew the country and could

188

read sign, which, in fact, Ben could also have done but he was satisfied to allow the cowman to do it, and he only occasionally dismounted to assure himself Clavenger was a good tracker.

He was. By midnight with a hint of a chill in the air Clavenger abruptly halted looking eastward. His son read the older man's mind. "Parallel with home."

Clavenger nodded and resumed walking ahead of his horse watching the ground. Clete slouched along with little to say even when Ben approached him.

His annoyance was justified, they were going pretty much back the way he and Ben had ridden before reaching the Clavenger place. Clete brightened slightly when Ben said, "He's headin' for country he knows."

Clete nodded. "Papago?"

Clavenger halted with the chill turning to cold, mounted and led off a-horseback without speaking. Ben and the blacksmith exchanged a look. Clete said, "I could eat the rear end out of a bear."

Ben was also hungry. Probably the Clavengers were also.

A wolf howled at the three-quarter moon and a band of foraging coyotes passed, hurrying and yapping at the same time.

Some other animal made a noise: a horse, and it was not far southward from the direction the pursuers were riding. Clavenger halted again and swung to the ground. Aaron caught the reins. Ben and Clete got down to stretch their legs.

This time the cowman was not gone very long. When he soundlessly appeared out of the darkness he was shaking his head. Clete spoke aside to the sheriff. "Another ghost story?"

Clavenger came up and pointed south-easterly. "Changed direction again." He did not mention the horse they had heard but went directly to his mount, swung across leather and altered course so as to veer away from the tracks they had been following.

Clete rode up beside him. "Wasn't that a horse?"

The older man replied cryptically. "A yearling surrounded by a band of coyotes. I scairt 'em off."

It became obvious to Ben that the cowman had something on his mind that troubled him. When Aaron rode up beside his father all the older man said was, "I wish he'd stole a different horse. That one can reach the yard before we can."

Ben eased up in his saddle. Clete leaned to say, "He's not that crazy, goin' back where there's people."

Ben offered no reply. Unlike the blacksmith he had experience with outlaws. It had taught him one thing; they were unpredictable.

A mile or so along Ben told Clete the outlaw needed food among other things, and if he didn't know the country — or even if he did — the nearest place where he could get what he needed, plus a fresh horse, was the Clavenger yard.

191

Aaron's father had difficulty restraining himself. He knew what Indians and renegades did to women, to anyone they caught by surprise. Eventually, he sent Aaron on ahead with orders to only go as far until he could see the yard, see a horse tied there, and return.

Clete rolled his eyes, which Ben saw and ignored. Aaron Clavenger hadn't impressed him as someone who would do as his father had ordered if he saw anything in the yard that implied trouble.

The horses were tired, their hind feet dragged, otherwise Ben was certain Clavenger would have picked up the gait. Some men still would have, and the result would be ending up on foot when wind-broke horses collapsed.

The chill had been increasing for several hours. Ben made a guess that dawn was no more than a couple of hours away. He was tired, so was Clete, neither'd had rest for more than twenty-four hours. They hadn't eaten either, things which combined affected men's alertness, and they might not have heard the very faint but distinctive sound of a gun shot.

The result was not at all what they expected. Carl Clavenger did not rowel his animal over into a run. Ben made an observation to Clete the cowman could not hear, he was fifty feet ahead. "Hard of hearin' sure as hell."

Clete did not respond, he slouched along watching Clavenger's back. When they were closer but with still several miles to go, Clete spoke aside to the sheriff. "If it'd been me I wouldn't have sent his son ahead." He offered no reason for this observation. He did not have to, Ben nodded understanding.

Clavenger reined back until the men from Papago were on each side of him. He said, "If that's him up yonder he must be a real desperate man."

Ben said, "He is, an' another thing, he's got to be as tough as old leather. We ain't let up long enough for him to rest or sleep."

"You reckon it's him, Sheriff?"

Ben replied warily. "If it ain't, who else would it be?"

Clavenger did not respond. He rode erectly, his lined and weathered face rigidly fixed. Ben looked and looked away. Whoever was at the yard, if the cowman caught him, Ben wouldn't want to see what was left afterwards. He had come to manhood among the variety of frontiersmen he was riding beside. Their laws, like their principles, were very simple. Violators died before sundown.

They eventually came upon a solitary horse that had been sleeping hip-shot. It made no move to get clear. The riders passed it within a distance of about a hundred feet. The old cowman said, "Wore out sick. Take six months for it to get back to feelin' good. It'll be the horse Jimminy seen the son of a bitch abandon."

There was no light showing and no sound as they got close enough to make out buildings. Clavenger did not pick up the gait. He rode as stiff as a ramrod, his mouth pulled flat. All the way to the corral behind the barn his head moved. As he swung off several using animals in the corral came over to investigate. Clavenger paused before saying, "We left four head. There's still four head. He ain't gone again."

That bothered the lawman and the blacksmith, but what bothered Carl Clavenger was something closer. As he led up through the barn he said, "Where's Shep? In ten years no one's ever come close without him lettin' us know."

He stopped just inside the barn's doorless wide opening to lean and gaze toward the house. It was the sheriff who caught movement northerly near the end of the yard. He brushed the cowman's arm and pointed.

Clavenger looked hard before speaking. "Aaron's horse." He pulled back from the opening. "Somethin's dead wrong," he muttered. Ben and Clete agreed without saying so.

Off in the east a faint streak of pearl-grey light appeared. Dawn would be along directly, with sunlight. Clavenger faced his companions. "You boys mind the front an' the yard. I'm goin' to sneak around back." He paused. "Don't shoot until you're damned sure it ain't Aaron."

After the cowman had left, Clete spoke in a whisper to the sheriff. "If Aaron's around I'll lay money he's face down."

Ben eased up where the cowman had been and leaned to peek out. With marginally better light and visibility he studied the front of the house. There was no movement. The hush was almost palpable.

Clete stepped forward to also look; as he pulled back he said, "If he's in there an' that old man catches him, he won't die sudden. You see his face?"

Ben nodded and leaned again to look out. A door opened and closed. Clete said, "Bunkhouse. You expect the old man's riders got back?"

Ben had no idea, but it seemed likely that if they had there would have been more than one gun shot. He remembered Clavenger saying his hired riders were moving cattle to spring feed up north, the implication was that they wouldn't be back soon.

That noisy door opened and closed again. Ben made a good guess. "Jimminy; likely scairt peeless an' stayin' inside. Openin' the door now an' then to peek out."

Clete built a theory around that. "The son of a bitch has got to be in the house, then."

"If he is, Clavenger'll get him."

Moments later three gun shots erupted, one slow the other two as fast as someone could tug jack and let the hammer drop.

Clete murmured worriedly, "Clavenger — he either nailed the son of a bitch or got nailed."

Ben was restless. He peered toward the house again, neither saw nor heard anything and faced around. "I'm goin' over behind the house," he said.

The reaction was instantaneous. "Not alone you ain't."

The corralled using stock lined up like crows on a fence watching the pair of two-legged creatures slip southerly along the back of the barn, hesitate, then spring swiftly to the protection of another building, much smaller, which smelled faintly of something sweet, and smoke. It had been built of logs with the meeting places of every pair of logs thoroughly chinked so that air could neither get in or get out.

The next southerly building was the bunkhouse. It was larger, also of logs, had an overhang out front with a bench, and in back had another overhang which protected the area where a blue-rimmed white wash basin was suspended from a nail beside which was a towel. There were two steps from where the clean-up area was and the ground. They took plenty of time before making another dash. The distance between the smokehouse and the bunkhouse was a good seventy feet.

They made it and paused to suck air. Clete peered southward. The next log building, clearly a well house, was smaller than either of the preceding buildings and had been purposefully placed within easy walking distance of the house. The difficulty here was that the distance between the bunkhouse and the well house was something like 300 feet, far enough for two freight wagons with four-horse hitches to pass through with room to spare.

Clete was as tense as a coiled spring while considering their next rush when that door opened and slammed again. He rose in the air as though propelled by invisible force. Ben slammed back against the log wall. Clete hissed enough curses to turn the air blue. Ben said, "Let's go back. Whoever's in the bunkhouse'll know more'n we do."

Clete remained furious. "I'll strangle him. What's the point of openin' an' closin' the damned door anyway!"

Ben replied curtly as he moved around the blacksmith to peer northward, "If it's Clavenger's idiot — "

"I'll strangle him anyway," the blacksmith retorted as they both eased back the way they had come, took down several deep breaths and with six-guns in hand moved along the back wall.

In some circumstances there were advantages to poor visibility. The sun was coming but it would be a while yet.

They inched along the north wall of the bunkhouse. Ben stopped only to tell the blacksmith to put the damned Colt in its holster, which Clete reluctantly did.

At the northeast corner they stopped to listen. The only sound was a busy wood-rat and that noise stopped the moment Ben, in front, leaned to peek around the corner. At the same moment the bunkhouse door was opened and slammed again.

They had to waste time being assured

the slammed door had not alarmed anyone.

Clete whispered. "Let me go first."

Ben put his arm out, hard. "You go back where the washstand is. Rattle your gun barrel along the wall when you're ready. I'll come in from out front. Whoever he is we'll have him between us."

Clete departed, but not enthusiastically and Ben stood poised just beyond the small porch of the bunkhouse. It seemed to him to take more time than was necessary, but eventually the blacksmith ran his handgun up and down the back wall logs.

Ben didn't rush, he moved as soundlessly as he could to reach the overhang door, gripped the latch hard with his left hand, held his six-gun cocked and poised in his right hand. When he opened the door he did so with sufficient force for it to strike the inside wall.

11

The New Day

JIMMINY was so frightened he dropped the shotgun. It went off with deafening sound. Clete jumped ahead, rammed his gun barrel into the small man's middle so hard Jimminy stumbled backwards and fell. He cringed without making any attempt to arise.

Ben leathered his sidearm, kicked the shotgun aside, got a fistful of the terrified cripple's shirt and yanked him to his feet.

Clete swore; that shotgun blast would have aroused anyone within a quarter of a mile.

Jimminy had saliva down his chin as Ben pushed him toward a table with several benches. The small man sat down shaking from head to foot. Any other time Ben would have felt sorry for him. Frightened words tumbled from the crippled, short man.

"I thought you was him. He hit me. I come in here an' barred the door. When I got the shotgun loaded I peeked out a couple of times but he warn't in sight."

Clete rummaged until he found the nearly empty bottle of whiskey, poured some into a glass, handed it to Jimminy and said, "Down it!"

Jimminy obeyed without taking his eyes off the blacksmith. He was more afraid of Clete than the sheriff. Right at this moment Clete looked more deadly than the sheriff. When Jimminy put the glass aside he shuddered. He was obviously not accustomed to liquor, but within moments the shaking stopped. The terror in his eyes, though, did not lessen.

Ben sat on a bench. "Where is he?" he asked and got an answer both he and the blacksmith expected.

"At the house. He come in the dark.

I recognized Mister Aaron's horse an' figured it was him."

Clete and the sheriff exchanged a look. Jimminy should have known better. Clete's anger was somewhat mollified when he too yanked a bench around and sat down facing the short man. "He was the same feller you watched rig out Aaron's horse?"

Jimminy vigorously nodded.

"Was there trouble at the house?" Ben asked and Jimminy shook his head. "I ain't sure what happened after he knocked me down in the barn, but when I come around wasn't nobody around. I went out back, caught Mister Aaron's horse an' cared for it. It was just about ready to fall down." For the first time there was anger in Jimminy's voice. "He had no right to treat that horse that way. He's a real friendly horse. Him'n me been friends since he was a colt."

Jimminy was calmer, the men from Papago had heard all they wanted to know. Ben arose, picked up the

204

scattergun, broke it and ejected both shells, one of which was expended. He leaned it aside as he said, "Stay in here," to Jimminy. "Don't reload the shotgun. Just stay quiet in here. You understand?"

Jimminy vigorously nodded. He asked if the sheriff meant to go over to the house. When Ben nodded Jimminy said, "Someone got shot."

Ben nodded. "You just stay in here. Don't go outside an' don't plug loads into that scattergun."

Jimminy arose. He was a good head shorter than either of the other men, and now he smiled widely. He put the sheriff in mind of a dog that's been scolded or hit. If Jimminy'd had a tail he would have wagged it.

They left the bunkhouse by the rear door. It was cold but with daylight, visibility was excellent. As Clete sidled along the west side of the bunkhouse he said, "If he's watchin' he'll sure as hell see us when we run for the well house."

Ben leaned around until he could see the house. It had a foreboding appearance in its silence that reached him.

Clete made another observation. "He heard that damned shotgun sure as hell, so he knows someone's out here . . . I wish to hell it hadn't got bright so soon."

Ben made no comment to either of the blacksmith's remarks. As he stiffened back he said, "I'd give a pretty to know the result of that gunshot an hour back."

"If he shot Clavenger then it'd be quiet like it is. If Clavenger shot him, he'd have let us know."

Ben agreed with that logic without speaking. He already knew that on the far side of the yard, a good four or five hundred feet from where he and the blacksmith were standing, there were other outbuildings, something that looked like a granary as well as a three-cornered smithy and a small building with a long, pole tie rack out front, which would be the harness room and saddlery.

It was while they were considering options that an argument erupted at the house. If it hadn't been utterly still they couldn't have made out as much as they did. First a man snarled, "Leave him be!" That was followed by a voice both men from Papago recognized. Fanny Wallace spoke sharply. "He needs care. I ain't goin' to stand here an' do nothin'!"

"You old witch, you touch him an' I'll blow your head off." This threat was followed by an even louder demand. "Woman, you show me where he keeps his cash box. I ain't goin' to ask you again!"

This time the female voice was deeper and blunt. "I told you — we don't keep no cash. We pay the riders when they go with us up to the bank in Benchmark. An' that's the gospel truth!"

Ben leaned to address Clete. "I guess he got Clavenger."

Clete nodded. "Where in hell is Aaron?"

Ben shrugged. He had no idea where Clavenger's son was but it seemed likely he'd be close by somewhere.

Once more the snarling voice came clearly to the men behind the bunkhouse. "You stay where I can see you. He don't need no basin of water. I said *stay*!"

The old woman's retort was both waspish and challenging. "Shoot me, you no good son of a bitch! Shoot me like you shot my boy back on the Papago road. He's all I had left in the world."

There was a long period of silence before the snarly voice spoke again. "You come out of that kitchen with a weapon, you old witch, an' I'll shoot him again, then you!" The voice changed slightly. "If you don't want him shot again, missus, you better show me where the money is!"

This time when Abigail Clavenger spoke there was an edge to her voice. "If you got a brain in your head you'll get away from here. You heard that shot from the yard. There'll be others out there. My son and others."

This time the snarly voice sounded almost humourlessly amused. "There can be a damned army out there, old woman, with you'n her — an' him — hostages in here they ain't goin' to do anythin'. For the last time — where is the cache?"

Clete muttered under his breath. "Tell him, woman! Tell him!"

The cowman's wife replied in a strong, firm tone of voice. "Come along, I'll show you where we got some money, an' where my jewelry an' gold watch is."

Again there was silence. Ben nudged the blacksmith. "I'll make the run. Likely him'n her are movin' clear. If you see anythin' shoot it!"

Behind them and around front the bunkhouse door was opened and slammed again. Clete rolled his eyes. Ben waited a long moment before making his dash. He halted behind the well house waiting for whatever might come. Nothing did, his guess about the renegade following Abigail Clavenger away from the parlour was correct. He motioned for Clete to join him and the blacksmith was poised to do so when a wolf sounded off westerly and was answered by another wolf out somewhere in the east side of the yard. Clete straightened up as Ben raised a hand for the blacksmith to stay where he was.

Neither wolf call had sounded convincing to men who had been listening to wolves most of their lives.

Ben eased along the well house wall until he had a good view of the front of the house. A pair of white curtains hung in front of the only front-wall window. They were half open. Ben had noticed them before. The shade porch and its scattering of chairs was also as he remembered them. The distance between the well house and the porch was not far, he could close the distance in moments.

He balanced his chances, which seemed mostly to depend on how long the renegade would be diverted by Clavenger's wife, and they had been silent a relatively long time

Clete suddenly made the run, bumped the sheriff breathing hard as he said, "Them wasn't wolves . . . Aaron?"

Ben's reply was curt. "Two of 'em on opposite sides of the yard?"

The sound of a chair, some heavy piece of furniture, being knocked over came distinctly to the men behind the well house. It was followed with an angry statement. "You old witch, you try that again an' I'll use the knife on you. Get away from him! Get over by the window an' stay there!"

Ben considered the west side of the house. Clete said, "Wait until he's interested in somethin' else," but Ben could make out the scrawny silhouette of Fanny Wallace where she stood with her back to the window. It seemed unlikely that if the renegade was elsewhere in the parlour, he would be unable to see the well house on the west side of the yard.

He told Clete to watch the window and ran. Nothing happened. This side of the mainhouse was roughly forty feet from north to south. Ben saw one window, guessed it was a bedroom and when he got close, crouched along beneath the sill.

Those wolves sounded again, both leaving echoes on each side of the house, southward.

Ben flattened. Whoever the 'wolves' were they were also seeking to get behind the houses and, assuming one might be old Clavenger's son, and the second one no one Ben would know or who would know him, Ben's position was not enviable. In daylight quick-triggered men — and that was his impression of Aaron Clavenger — would shoot at anyone they saw skulking in the area of the house.

He looked back. Clete was standing in a slight crouch looking westerly. Ben looked too but saw nothing. He did not move, to do so would make his position detectable. He swore to himself. The feeling was about like a bug fixing to be pinned to a wall. As Clete had observed, a little nightfall would have been a great help.

Inside the house another argument erupted, this time between the large, deep-voiced woman and the renegade. She said, "I won't let him die! We been husband'n wife close to forty years."

Fanny Wallace chimed in using her same theme as before. "Ain't you satisfied with killin' my boy? That man's as helpless as a kitten."

The response was delayed but it eventually came. "Whoever's out there'll hear the shot that takes the old man out. They'll know I mean business."

"They know that already," the old woman retorted. "Mister, if you figure to get clear you'd better not make things no worse. This here is hang-rope country. Take me hostage but don't hurt Mister Clavenger no more."

The renegade spat out his response.

"I had you hostage once, an' you tripped a horse so's I'd leave you. I know how you got here. I know that Papago lawman's out there."

Fanny Wallace sarcastically said, "Sprout wings. That's the only way you'll get away from here alive."

The renegade's reply was brusque. "You two'll go with me to the barn, one in front, one behind. Whoever's out there won't shoot women."

Fanny waspishly said, "Don't bet on it. Mister, you don't stand the chance of a snowball in hell. They're out there, you're forted up in here an' the barn's a long hike. Use your brain — if you got one — give up."

The renegade did not reply. Giving up would not prevent him from being taken to the nearest tree and left dangling there.

Fanny made another comment that Ben heard word for word. "Whiskey won't help."

The hurled bottle missed the old woman by inches, broke the glass window and came to rest in the yard beyond the porch.

Clete groaned, genuine glass windows were not nearly impossible to come by but they cost as much as some men made in six months. Clete did not have a glass window in his shop nor where he bedded down.

Ben sidled by inches toward the south corner of the log wall. He waited briefly, removed his hat and peeked around. Aaron was inching along the back wall in the direction of the steps leading to the porch where the rear door was.

That, Ben told himself, accounted for one of the wolves. It also reinforced Ben's earlier conviction that old Clavenger's son was likely to act without thinking.

He was straightening back when a cold pistol barrel dented the side of his neck. He did not move but someone else did. Clete softly said, "Drop that gun you hairy-faced bastard. *Drop it!*"

Ben turned. Clete had come around

from the front of the house. He had seen the stalker coming from the west. The man was thick, burly and unshaven. He let his Colt drop.

Ben asked who he was. The answer was enlightening. "Top-hand for Mister Clavenger. I come back early to tell him we're missin' some cattle. Rustler up north sure as hell. Who are you?"

Ben did not answer, he leaned, saw how close Aaron was to the steps and hissed. Aaron jerked straight up cocking his handgun. Ben spoke quietly. "It's me, Sheriff Walls. We got your hairy-faced rider around here. Come along an' join us. Be real quiet."

The top-hand was studying Clete. "Ain't you the blacksmith down at Papago?" he asked.

Clete's reply was thick with exasperation. "Yes I am, when I'm not ridin' with Sheriff Walls all over Hell's half acre."

Ben prevented any further conversation by saying, "He's in the house an' I think Mister Clavenger's been shot."

Aaron straightened up. Ben spoke directly to him. "You go bustin' in there an' your mother'll be cryin' by sundown. Whoever he is, he's quick with a gun."

The bearded man said, "Four to one. Two in front, two in back an' we rush the house."

Even Clete groaned at that statement.

"He's got two women an' Mister Clavenger. We got nothin' but the ability to kill him the minute he shows his head, an' he's no fool."

The bearded man, smarting over the scorn shown for his proposal, scowled at the sheriff. "So what do we do?"

"Set down for a spell," the sheriff replied. "He ain't slept in more'n two days. He hadn't eaten either, until he got into the house, but it'd take too long to starve him out anyway. But one more night without sleep might do it." Ben looked directly at the top-hand. "Break into the house before dawn. If we're lucky he'll be dead to the world."

The top-hand said, "One way or another he'll sure as hell be dead."

Clete got restless. So did Aaron. What particularly bothered Aaron was when one of those sporadic arguments broke out. They could hear every word. The hotter the argument got the more upset Aaron Clavenger became. Clete mentioned food which diverted the rangeman and Aaron Clavenger. Ben eyed his friend. He hadn't noticed it before and maybe it went with his trade, but regardless of how bad a situation was, the blacksmith could be relied upon to mention being hungry.

The top-hand and Aaron discussed rustled cattle. During their conversation the top-hand mentioned the other riders being at a line camp about fifteen miles from the yard, a place called Piney Woods. Any idea the men from Papago had of reinforcements arriving was forgotten. They didn't need more men, they needed a miracle.

During Ben's life miracles had been in short supply. He considered the burly, bewhiskered rangeman. He had a feeling however that when this situation ended it would not end as the top-hand wanted it to, in a blazing gun battle.

Clete slept. Ben also did but lightly. He had little confidence in Aaron Clavenger and about an equal amount in the top hand after that remark about charging the house head on.

Jimminy arrived burdened with food from the bunkhouse. Before he reached the others he began a well-meaning but clumsy justification for not remaining in the bunkhouse as he'd been told to do.

Ben shook his head. Jimminy had crab-walked from the bunkhouse to the west wall of the mainhouse carrying sacks of food. If the forted up renegade had been anywhere near the window he could have shot the simple-minded cripple.

As Clete ate he made a suggestion. "He might be sleepin'. I'll sneak under the winder and raise up an' look in."

No one objected so Clete finished

eating and worked his way toward the only window in the west wall and with the others watching, removed his hat and very slowly straightened up.

What happened none of them expected. An ancient house cat half as large as a small dog had been sleeping on the sill in sunshine. When Clete's head arose above the sill the startled cat sprang up, every hair erect, spit, hissed and yowled as though it had a killer dog in sight.

Clete dropped down, scuttled back to the others and scowled at Aaron. "I didn't see no cat when we was here before."

"You wasn't in my folks' bedroom. He sleeps in there, has for years. My ma found him starvin' in Benchmark years ago an' brought him home."

Clete found scraps of food left, ate them and wouldn't look at young Clavenger.

Ben would have laughed under

different circumstances. He might have now if one of those arguments hadn't erupted in the parlour. Fanny Wallace's easily identified voice shrilled loudly. "A man who'd take a woman's weddin' ring's got to be no better'n a crawlin' varmint."

The renegade hung fire briefly before replying: "If you was wearin' one I wouldn't make you pull it off, I'd cut off your damned finger!"

Fanny lashed out again. "You know what you done, you brainless bastard? You wasted too much time robbin' the Clavengers an' shootin' the old man. If you'd had as much sense as Gawd give a goose you'd have done your robbin' an' eatin' and lit out of here like the Devil was chasin' you." Fanny paused, then said, "He is, for a blessed fact. He's after you an' he's goin' to get you!"

The renegade's reply was not as loudly offered as his previous one had been, which made the listeners outside willing to believe that this time he meant exactly what he said when he told the old woman if she opened her mouth one more time he'd gut her like a chicken with the same knife she'd sneaked out of the kitchen.

12

Two Long Days

THE cat's squalling brought prolonged silence in the parlour. Ben gestured for his companions to move swiftly around the corner to the rear of the house.

They barely made it and, although the renegade looked out from beside the inner sill and saw no men, he did see where they had been eating.

He returned to the parlour eyeing the women. Fanny Wallace said it again. "Mister, you waited too long."

Surprisingly the renegade did not show anger when he replied. "Maybe, but I ain't whipped yet." He gestured toward Abigail Clavenger. "You, open the door, don't go out, stand in the doorway and yell to 'em I'll trade you'n the old scarecrow for a saddled horse brought to the house." Evidently the large woman did not move because an edge crept into the man's voice when he also said, "*Do it!* I'll kill the old man. *Do it!*"

The men behind the house eased back along the west side as they heard the porch door being opened. A man's voice said, "That's far enough. Now tell 'em!"

Aaron's mother called out the message, hesitated and repeated it. They heard the door close as she went back inside. Jimminy would have spoken but Clete saw it coming and clamped a large hand over the crippled man's mouth. Jimminy cringed as though he'd been struck. Clete raised a rigid finger in Jimminy's face. "Don't open your mouth again. No matter what, don't you open it."

Ben nudged the blacksmith, diverted him by saying, "We get back to the barn." He briefly rested a hand on Jimminy's shoulder, gave him a slight tug.

Returning as they had come was more difficult because there were now three more bodies to seek concealment behind the sheds.

The sun was high, men sweated, there was barn shade ahead which extended over the pole corrals out back.

Aaron walked up on Ben's heels. He was peering back at the front of the house. Ben reached, roughly pushed the younger man back and followed Clete as they scuttled from the well house to the bunkhouse and from there to the rear of the barn.

Jimminy wasn't built for hurrying but he did his best. When they were safely behind the barn Ben slapped the cripple lightly on the shoulder and if looks had meaning, Jimminy's expression indicated that he would have followed the lawman until Hell froze over and for two days on the ice.

A man's voice called from the house. "Sheriff? You bring the horse over here, an' Sheriff, one bad move an' I'll kill all three of 'em in the house."

Aaron jumped forward. Clete grabbed him, spun around and hurled him away. As he'd done before, he raised a rigid finger. "You do somethin' crazy one more time an' I'll split your damned head!"

The burly top-hand glared at Clete from sunk-set small pale eyes but did nothing.

Jimminy cringed at the moment of violence, moving toward the rear barn opening. Ben came up to him with a question.

"How many horses in the corral an' the barn?"

Jimminy answered without hesitation. Child-like he loved animals, cared for them well, knew them by names he invented.

"Five in the corral countin' Mister Aaron's horse that feller come back on. Two inside, one's a mare fixin' to calve. The other one's Mister Clavenger's special horse."

As the others edged closer to the

doorless opening and went inside Ben held Jimminy back. "Is there a bucker or maybe an up-an'-over horse among 'em?"

Jimminy looked shocked. "Mister Clavenger don't keep spoilt horses."

Ben tried a different approach. "A horse don't have to be bad to be a halter-puller or maybe one that bites."

Jimminy agreed. "I had one once that'd bite your butt when you turned to shove a foot into the stirrup. Mister Clavenger liked him, he was savvy and tough, but when he bit Mister Clavenger he said we'd trail him to Benchmark an' trade him off. I told him the horse'n me was friends. He said we'd keep him if I could break him from bitin' folks. I fixed him. Anyone went to mount him I'd say shorten the off-side rein. That way he couldn't turn his head. You see?"

Ben nodded and smiled. "You still got him, Jimminy?"

"No. That was when I was young. Last year we found him dead under a tree." Jimminy looked away and sniffled.

Ben patted his shoulder. "Like losin' a friend. I know. Jimminy, out of six horses don't you have one that bucks hard or goes over backward, or somethin'?"

Jimminy's eyes brightened. "One. That big sorrel mare in the corral. You can drive her anywhere, pull any load, but you can't ride her more'n a hunnert yards. We don't ride her. Mister Clavenger keeps her because she's so willin' in harness."

Clete poked his head out the doorless opening. "You goin' to palaver out there all day? That son of a bitch is goin' to start frettin' directly."

Ben and Jimminy entered the barn. Ben singled out the bearded, burly top-hand. "Jimminy was tellin' me about a sorrel mare in the corral."

The burly man said, "What about her?"

"She can pull twice her weight."

"That's right. We got no other animal

that's as hell for stout. You want to pull somethin'?"

Aaron, who had been listening, came over as the sheriff asked the top-hand about riding the sorrel mare. Aaron spoke before the burly man could. "There's been a dozen try over the years." His face brightened. "Hell! That'd work. She stands good bein' saddled an' bridled an' she leads good." Aaron looked at the top-hand. "Bring her in. That son of a bitch won't get fifty yards before she bogs her head, an' Sheriff, that old girl can pop half the buttons off your shirt when she takes to you."

The top-hand got a shank and went out back to the corral. Clete was sceptical. He watched the mare being led inside. At close-handling she did exactly what was expected of her. She weighed close to 1,300 pounds and was muscled up where a lot of horses didn't have places for that much power.

She was as gentle as a kitten. Ben scratched her back. She responded by jerkily wiggling her nose.

Even when Jimminy brought a saddle, blanket and bridle she stood patiently to be rigged out. Ben took the reins, turned her twice, led her toward the front barn opening and back. She walked along as any broke saddle animal would.

He handed the reins to Clete, went up front and called to the house. "All right, mister, we got your animal ready."

The reply was belated but eventually it came. "Lead it out where I can see it."

Clete led the mare out into sunlight. She stood relaxed.

The renegade called again. "Sheriff? This is what you got to do. First off, you'n them with you pitch your weapons out where I can see 'em. Then they come out'n stand in front of the barn so's I can keep an eye on 'em. An' when I come out I'll have the women in front of me. Don't none of you do anything you shouldn't. I'd as leave kill those women as look at 'em. You understand?"

To show that he not only understood but intended to obey Sheriff Walls unbuckled his shell-belt with its holstered Colt and let it fall.

The fugitive clapped approvingly. "Good. Now the others."

Inside the barn Aaron did not offer to drop his belt and gun until Clete started toward him. The burly top-hand stepped between them. Clete did not hesitate. He hit the burly man with the speed of a striking snake, low in the soft parts. The top-hand bent double, grimacing. Clete shoved him away and faced young Clavenger. "Get rid of the belt an' gun," he said shortly, and Aaron obeyed.

Ben waited until the top-hand was able to stand erect, before calling to the house. "We're disarmed."

"You lead the horse over here, an' if you're figurin' on double-crossin' me remember, I'll have the women. You understand, Lawman?"

Ben understood. "Just get on the horse and clear out of here."

"Bring it over!"

Ben led the big mare. She followed like a dog. As they were approaching the stairs leading up to the porch the door opened a crack. Ben couldn't see the renegade, both women were in the doorway, but the man spoke. His voice was pitched slightly high. "One bad move, lawman an' I'll get you too."

Ben stood with the mare saying nothing. The renegade shoved Abigail Clavenger out first using the barrel of his six-gun. She winced, otherwise she stepped out looking stonily at Sheriff Walls.

The men lined up in front of the barn seemed to be scarcely breathing. Clavenger's dog, Shep, who had been hiding under the porch poked his head out and mistakenly thought it was safe. He crawled out, shook and wagged his tail. What drove him back under the porch was when Fanny Wallace was jammed in the back too, and swore a blue streak. Any blow over the kidneys was painful. Shep immediately disappeared back under the porch.

She stumbled toward the larger woman, recovered and would have said more but the man behind her cocked his hand gun. She looked straight ahead, lips flat and speechless.

The renegade remained in parlour shadows as he said, "Lawman, remember, you or any of them bastards in front of the barn so much as blink an' the killin' begins."

Ben answered dryly, "Get on the horse an' get the hell out of here."

The renegade appeared in the doorway. He didn't have one six-gun, he had two; the second one belonged to Carl Clavenger. He hesitated before growling at the women. They moved toward the steps like sleep-walkers. At the top step he said, "Slow, real slow."

They descended one foot at a time. The man was so close behind them Ben could see little more than shoulders in a filthy shirt and booted feet in wrinkled trousers.

When the women stopped the man told them to approach the mare on the left side, to stay close together, and as they moved like stilt-walkers, faces expressionless, Ben held out the reins.

The man said, "Sheriff, you walk along the east side of the house. Out a ways so's if anyone gets reckless I can see you."

Ben handed the reins to Fanny Wallace. They exchanged a steady look before the sheriff started away in the direction of the east side log wall of the house.

There was not a sound.

The renegade shoved the women to one side, grabbed the reins, jammed his left foot into the stirrup and rose up to settle over leather with his right hand moving. His left hand had the reins as well as the other six-gun.

The renegade yanked the mare around and hooked her as hard as he could. The shock and pain startled the mare so much that she bounded into the air and lit down running.

The people in the yard were riveted. As the mare raced past Ben he saw her throw her head to get the bit between her teeth. Fifty feet onward with the renegade crouched low, the mare rose up and came down stiff-legged. The renegade, leaning forward, almost went off over the mare's head. He let out a roaring curse, dropped the right-hand gun and grabbed the saddle horn.

The mare's second buck was high. She came down stiff-legged and her rider lost his hat. He now grabbed the horn with both hands and hooked her again hard, as though he expected that would make her run, which might have happened with most horses but not this one.

He could not pull her head up. She had the bit tightly between her teeth. Nothing short of a derrick could have got her head up. The third time she bucked the renegade lost a stirrup.

He was groping for it when she went

high and came down hard enough to make the ground shake. He lost the other stirrup and one rein, but his grip on the horn was vice-like.

Clete and Aaron ran to their weapons. Fanny Wallace raced for the parlour and returned with an old Sharps army rifle which had been above the fireplace. It wasn't loaded, hadn't been loaded for fifteen years. She threw it to her shoulder and pulled the trigger. Nothing happened. She flung the gun aside, stood ramrod-stiff on the porch as the men in front of the barn found their weapons.

Ben was next to the log wall when the mare bogged her head and bucked, sunfishing from left to right. It was doubtful that the best bucking horse rider in New Mexico could have stayed on top and the renegade, already badly battered, went off like a rag doll.

He scrabbled in the dirt, twisted and emptied his six-gun in the direction of the men running toward him from the barn. One man went down.

Ben lunged for the weapon the renegade had lost, was sliding toward it when a withering fusillade of gunshots erupted. Ben retrieved the gun, rolled up to his knees bringing the gun to bear when the renegade rolled and jerked each time a bullet struck him.

Fanny Wallace yelled from the east edge of the porch. "That's enough! You want mince meat?"

The firing stopped.

Ben was the first to the body. Whoever the renegade was it was doubtful that his friends, if he had any, or his mother would have recognized him.

Abigail Clavenger approached the corpse wooden-faced, leaned, rummaged in a pocket, got her wedding ring, put it on her finger and ignored everything as she walked purposefully toward the house.

While the others crowded around the body Ben looked in the direction of the barn. A man was facedown no more than fifty or sixty feet from the building. Ben walked back. Clete turned to follow. On the way he handed the sheriff his six-gun, which Ben holstered without slackening his stride nor looking away from the figure ahead.

It was Jimminy. One of the renegade's bullets had struck him directly over the heart.

Abigail Clavenger appeared on the porch to call the sheriff. As he walked toward her he was joined by Aaron, whose stride was longer. He reached the porch first and entered the house. His mother waited for the sheriff. When they were face to face Ben had no trouble recognizing the expression of fear. He went inside where Aaron was on his knees beside the big old leather couch where his father was lying.

Ben went close, saw the bloody bandage, told Aaron to fetch a basin of hot water and spoke to the wounded man. "Can you hear me, Mister Clavenger?"

The wounded man turned a drowsy

gaze and nodded.

The bullet had struck Clavenger in the hip, it was a gory mess but the bone had been spared. Ben looked up at Abigail. "He's lost a sight of blood."

Her reply was cryptic. "That man wouldn't let me do no more'n wrap a towel around the leg. Sheriff . . . ?"

Ben stood up. "I'm not a doctor, ma'am. I'd guess if he ain't lost too much blood he'll make it. But one thing I'm sure of — it'll be a long time before he straddles a horse."

The frozen-faced woman said, "I just want him alive."

Ben asked for whiskey, which was brought as Aaron returned with the basin of hot water. Ben motioned for Abigail to doctor the injury, leaned, lifted Clavenger's head and got three swallows of whiskey down him. Within moments Clavenger's colour improved and while his wife was washing the ragged wound Clavenger fell asleep — or passed out.

Outside, the top-hand had carried Jimminy to the bunkhouse. Jimminy didn't show much blood. He looked as though he were asleep. Clete was sitting by the bunk and addressed the sheriff. "How's the old woman?"

"All right."

"She come in here a while back, looked at Jimminy, busted out cryin' and run outside."

Ben nodded. Her fears for her son back in Papago would have been resurrected by the sight of Jimminy dead on his bunk.

The top-hand was outside rolling a smoke. He glanced at Ben, licked the quirley, popped it into his mouth and spoke around trickling smoke. "How's Mister Clavenger?"

"Hit in the hip. Lost a sight of blood. I'd guess he'll make it but he won't be up an' around for a long time."

The top-hand flicked ash. "Jimminy was harmless."

Ben nodded.

Clete came across the yard leading

the mare. He spoke briefly aside to the top-hand. "You folks ought to keep this critter. She done more'n all the rest of us."

The top-hand waited until Clete was gone before addressing the sheriff again. "I'm goin' to miss Jimminy."

The burly man hadn't impressed Ben as an individual who had either a nerve or sentiment in his body.

The top-hand ground out his smoke underfoot and said, "Well, I'll go drag that damned carrion out of the sun," and would have walked away but Ben asked what would be done with the dead man. The top-hand barely missed a stride as he replied, "If I had my way we'd drag the son of a bitch to a canyon an' roll him down it. But Missus Clavenger wouldn't stand for that. She's a Christian lady."

Ben entered the barn where Clete was off-saddling the big mare. He had scarcely got there when Fanny Wallace walked in. She ignored Clete and the mare, looked steadily at Ben and said,

"It's time for us to go, Sheriff."

Clete eyed the old woman. "We can't just up an' ride off."

She contradicted him. "Yes we can. If you don't want to come along I'll see if Miz Clavenger'll let me have a horse. I'll pay good for it. But I'm goin' back."

She walked out of the barn leaving the men looking after her. Clete surprised the sheriff when he said, "Her son. I don't think what she finds will make her feel better."

What surprised the sheriff was the degree of perception he'd heard in the blacksmith's voice.

An hour later the old woman came briskly across to the barn with the burly man. He brought in a horse from the corral, wordlessly helped her rig it out, handed her the reins — and smiled, something the men from Papago would not have thought he was capable of doing.

Abigail Clavenger told Ben and Clete she had refused pay for the horse, told them it was a proven using horse and also told them primly how much she appreciated what they had done. What she did not say was something she and her husband discussed the following winter: if the sheriff hadn't chased that renegade so relentlessly, what had happened to the Clavengers would not have happened.

Ben and Clete did not overtake Fanny Wallace until dusk when she had stopped to hobble the animal and let it graze while she sat on some rocks where she could see in all directions, and ate jerky.

When they come up, hobbled and off-saddled their animals not a word was said until the old woman offered jerky from a greasy bag — a gift to her from Abigail Clavenger — and told them she wouldn't need their company, and that she figured to travel fast.

They did not argue. In fact they said nothing because, with jerky, the longer a person chewed the bigger it got.

They left the rocks just short of

midnight, scarcely speaking except for when the old woman offered a canteen and they drank. Jerky cured with pepper was filling. It also required lots of water.

They rode steadily until dawn when Ben said they should rest the horses. The old woman would have protested but Clete shoved her away, hobbled her animal, removed the rigging, then got some molasses-cured tucked into one cheek and lay flat out with his hat covering his face.

Ben understood the old woman's sense of urgency and had a bad feeling concerning what she would find when she reached Papago. His worst expectations were both justified and unjustified.

They reached Papago with the sun slanting away. Clete and the sheriff told her which house belonged to the midwife then led the animals away to be cared for. Neither of them wanted to be present when she saw her son.

The liveryman came up to them to

say he was fixing to rig out the doctor's buggy and they looked blankly at him.

"He come through day afore yestiddy. Miz Lisabeth got him out of bed at the rooming-house to look at that young feller who got shot down the road. He'll be leavin' soon."

Clete ventured a question. "Is that shotfeller still alive?"

The liveryman nodded. "Come awful close though an' as I heard it'll be maybe until next summer before he's as good as new again."

They went up to the midwife's cottage. She met them in the parlour. She did not look like someone who had slept lately but she smiled. "A doctor was passing through and — "

"We know," Ben interrupted to say. "How's Justin?"

Her smile lingered. "If you never believed in prayer, Sheriff, let me tell you it works. I mean the doctor arriving when he did."

"Ma'am, how is Justin?"

"Weak and bad off but he'll make

it. His mother's with him. Would you like some coffee?"

Ben shook his head, went to a chair and sank down. He and Clete exchanged a look before the blacksmith said, "I got to get down to the shop."

From the doorway a woman's voice, softer than either the sheriff or the blacksmith had heard it before said, "Mister Morgan, my boy's goin' to mend."

Clete nodded from the doorway. "I'm right glad, ma'am."

The voice changed a little. "I told you, my name ain't ma'am, it's Fanny."

Clete nodded and fled. The old woman went as far as the door looking after Clete Morgan. "Good man," she murmured.

Ben and the midwife traded a look and Lisabeth broadly smiled. After the old woman had returned to the sick room Lisabeth said, "Sheriff — "

He cut her off. "Ben. Just plain Ben."

"Just-plain-Ben, I worried all the time you was gone. Was it bad?"

Ben arose eyeing the tall woman. "It's a long story, ma'am — Lisabeth."

She said, "I'd like to hear it. With Justin's mother here to mind him . . . do you own a buggy — Ben?"

"No . . . Lisabeth."

"I do, an' a gentle driving mare." She stood up facing the sheriff. "We could drive up country tomorrow afternoon an' you could tell me. I'll fetch along a hamper — Ben."

He stood like a cedar post gazing at her. After letting go a long silent breath he nodded. "I'd like that, ma'am."

She threw up her hands but before she could correct him again, he left the house.

THE END

FIGHTING RAMROD
Charles N. Heckelmann

Most men would have cut their losses, but Frazer counted the bullets in his guns and said he'd soak the range in blood before he'd give up another inch of what was his.

LONE GUN
Eric Allen

Smoke Blackbird had been away too long. The Lequires had seized the Blackbird farm, forcing the Indians and settlers off, and no one seemed willing to fight! He had to fight alone.

THE THIRD RIDER
Barry Cord

Mel Rawlins wasn't going to let anything stand in his way. His father was murdered, his two brothers gone. Now Mel rode for vengeance.

ARIZONA DRIFTERS
W. C. Tuttle

When drifting Dutton and Lonnie Steelman decide to become partners they find that they have a common enemy in the formidable Thurston brothers.

TOMBSTONE
Matt Braun

Wells Fargo paid Luke Starbuck to outgun the silver-thieving stagecoach gang at Tombstone. Before long Luke can see the only thing bearing fruit in this eldorado will be the gallows tree.

HIGH BORDER RIDERS
Lee Floren

Buckshot McKee and Tortilla Joe cut the trail of a border tough who was running Mexican beef into Texas. They stopped the smuggler in his tracks.